FemDom Short Stories

A Seductive and Vulgar Collection of Nine BDSM Short Stories (inspired by IRL events)

By: Alexandra Morris

About Alexandra Morris

Hey,

Thank you for choosing this book!

Are you interested in the FLR-lifestyle?
Searching for a mistress or Domina?

Great. You've come to the right place.

I'm a Femdom-enthusiast and self publishing
author. My mission is to spread the word
about Femdom far and wide.

You can visit my site alexandramorris.com for
more content, free books, blog articles and my
email newsletter.

When you have finished the book, please take
the time to leave an honest review!

I hope you will love the book ☺

Alexandra

Table of Contents

Story 1 - To Find a Mistress

As the subway doors closed, Caleb struggled to keep his eyes off the painted across from him. With his phone in his hand, swiping right on every woman that pops up with no second thoughts, Caleb's eyes were fixed on a woman dressed in a long coat and open-toe sandals, her toenails painted a shade of hot pink, and her foot irritably bouncing.

Caleb could feel a bead of sweat sliding down his cheek, his eyes shifting from the woman's heart-shaped face as she vigorously chewed gum, to her bouncing foot.

This was a typical day for Caleb Lautner.

While he never deemed himself unattractive per se, he wasn't exactly conventionally handsome. He was mostly shorter than the majority of women that he'd met, with his height at five-foot-six, and had always been quite the skinny guy. His body hadn't changed much since his mid-teens.

The subway doors opened, making the woman's hair whip behind her back long enough for Caleb to take a whiff of the woman's scent. An older woman, who was still seated on the bench, shot him a disapproving look, before he rushed outside, his eyes fixed on the woman's ass.

For an ordinary looking man like Caleb, with neither money nor skills to offer to a woman, it was nearly impossible to find a woman willing to cater to his insatiable desires...for free. Caleb had developed a habit of finding sex workers online, and although it was certainly better than nothing, he wanted someone to humiliate him because she wanted to.

He tossed his keys over the coffee table and plopped to his sofa, grabbing the TV remote next to him. His expressionless face lit up as the television turned on, loud groans echoing in the living room. It was a ninety-minute pornography movie titled *To Find a Mistress* about a man who'd finally found his dominatrix, and who ended up living in her sex dungeon.

The perfect happily ever after that Caleb had always dreamed of.

As much as it was easier to ease the edge off of loneliness with the hundreds of femdom movies he would browse and learn from, it was quickly becoming less satisfying. He'd tried everything. He'd bought the latest and most advanced flesh lights, he paid for and met new cam girls online, but the loneliness persisted and sexual frustration exacerbated.

Caleb only had a few friends, who weren't exactly the best wing men. However, Eric was his most good looking friend, and despite generally being a nuisance and a little bit of a moron, he was unequivocally a chick-magnet. There was a lot to learn from Eric, but Caleb rarely ever had the patience to tolerate him.

And just as he thought of his friend, his phone buzzed. Caleb turned to his phone beside him, glancing at the lit-up screen.

Think of the devil, he scoffed to himself.

Of course. It was another party. Being an introvert, Caleb never liked being around Eric's rowdy social circles. He wasn't exactly your typical awkward nerd, but it took him a lot of effort to put on a mask and keep his eyes on his drink at all times, lest any female guests call him a perfect for staring at a foot or two.

But at twenty-nine, it was now or never. He no longer had the luxury of time to loiter around and hope the dominatrix of his dreams will just pop up and knock at his door. He had to start looking, and there was no safer place for him to do that than the comfort of his pretty-boy friend's home.

His face lit up as he fantasized about finding his soulmate at the party, quickly grabbing the remote and turning off the porn before rushing upstairs to get dressed.

* * *

House music boomed from the massive speakers, uncomfortably thudding in Caleb's chest. He winced with the beat, and he couldn't help but knit his eyebrows with a beer can firmly held in his hand. He jerked upon feeling a vigorous pat on his back.

"My man!" Eric greeted, offering his fist for a bump.

Caleb straightened his expression and tried to feign a smile to no avail, still uncomfortable by how loud the music was in the room. He glanced at his friend's fist, awkwardly grabbing it and shaking his hand.

"Same old Caleb," Eric chuckled. "You good?"

"The music is atrocious," he replied nonchalantly.

"CJ!" Eric yelled, his voice sending a shrill down Caleb's spine. "Turn it down, will ya?"

The DJ complied.

Eric nudged him in the shoulder. "You still tapping the same ass?"

"What? Sam?" he shrugged. "We broke up six months ago."

And for good reason. Although Samantha and Caleb had so much in common – that was precisely the problem. Both of them wanted the other party to take control in bed, and they both just ended up frustrated and unfulfilled. It only took them a year to stop trying to convince themselves that their failure of a sex life wasn't everything, and that they otherwise got along. Until, of course, Sam cheated.

"Oh, shit. Sorry, dude."

"You already know. I told you five months ago," he continued with the same expressionless face.

"Damn, sorry. But hey, there's plenty of fish in the sea."

"I prefer women," he replied swiftly.

A female voice chuckled behind him. He turned around to see flawless woman, clad in a long slim-fit red dress. Her jet black hair fell along her shoulder in soft waves like a shiny scarf. He couldn't help but glance at her feet, and he smiled inwards after briefly feasting on her red-painted toenails that peeped out of her open-toe pumps.

He swallowed hard.

"Oh, Caleb, this is Carmen. Carmen, Caleb."

She seemed rather shy, her eyes flicking from his face to Eric's irritably. In a way, her shy demeanor made her seem more attractive and mysterious. She must have been at least five inches taller than him, her beautiful figure towering over his as she approached him to shake his hands.

"Wow," she exclaimed, gazing at his eyes.

His heart sunk.

"You're the only one at the party who hasn't offered me his fist for a bump," she joked.

Eric was already out of the picture, and Caleb suddenly felt his nervousness amplify. The two of the spent a good few minutes, each of them with a drink in hand. Caleb was visibly uncomfortable, and the Carmen suggested they sneak outside to have their drinks in a more quiet space.

She gestured to the garage door, and he followed with his heart racing against his chest. Her dress was tight, and mustering the strength not to stare at her ass was no easy feat, and he managed to sneak a glance before she turned around to shut the door behind them. Quietly, she climbed up the trunk of a 2009 Honda and patted the dust off her hands after she placed her beer can next to her. Her feet dangled, and she spun them in circles, staring at her own feet as she zoned out.

Her toes were slender and long, nicely painted with a shiny coat. Caleb could tell from the way she looked that she was a woman who took great care of herself. He took in a lungful of air, then broke the silence.

"So," he said. "How do you know Eric?"

"High school. You?"

"Same here," he nodded awkwardly, then glanced at the empty spot next to her, but she looked the other way, as though uncomfortable by the thought of him sitting so close to her. He grabbed bucket, turned it upside down, and took a seat.

"Cool, cool," he said.

Her gaze traveled to the door that led to the foyer, then she looked over her shoulder to glance at the garage door behind them. It appeared that she was either looking for a way out, or feeling unsafe with him.

"Hey, do you want me to leave?" he asked.

Carmen shot him a confused look, the corners of her lips slowly rising in a grin. "No," she said confidently, the look in her eyes fierce. She looked as though she had an entirely different personality from the girl he'd met in the living room.

He gulped. "Good to know," he nodded again, his eyes affixed on his drink.

"Are you always like this?" she asked, raising a brow.

"Quiet and awkward?" he inquired.

"A bit of a pushover," she answered with a grin.

His heart sunk. He felt a little humiliated, but the look on her face didn't seem to be all too hostile.

"A little nerdy," she continued. "And plenty submissive."

Caleb's eyes widened upon hearing a keyword that immediately aroused him. His half-empty beer can dropped to the floor, and he got up to avoid the puddle from staining his shoes.

"I'm sorry," he said with his back turned to her.

Behind him, he could hear her heels clang against the floor before she slowly approached him. Her arms snaked around his waist and she nestled her chin on his shoulder.

"That's a bit of a mess," she whispered, nibbling on his ear.

Her warm breath beat down his neck, sending ripples of euphoria throughout his body. He could feel her soft breasts pressing against his back, and he shut his eyes as he took a whiff of her scent.

"Someone will have to clean that up," she continued, her hands moving up and down his arms. "Besides, it's a bit of a waste, don't you think?"

"I..."

"Shhh," she silenced him. "Did I say you could speak?"

It all made little sense as to why a woman as gorgeous as Carmen would be immediately drawn to someone like Caleb. And although it crossed his mind that this could have been some sort of prank, he went along with it.

Running her hands up his torso, she stopped at his nipples and pinched hard, twisting them erect ever-so-slightly and smiling every time he let out a soft whimper. Caleb hadn't felt like himself in years.

For the first time ever, he didn't need to mask his flamboyance, seeing as it appeared to please Carmen.

With one hand pinching his nipple, the other slid down his torso to unbuckle his belt that she tossed across the garage space. He was sweating and his fingertips were shaky, and he could feel himself getting hard. She stuffed her hands down his boxers and let out a soft chuckle.

"Whoa, you're excited," she noted, lifting her fingers up to his mouth for him to lick.

He sucked his own juices off each of her fingers. She then praised him, "Good boy. Now, it's time to clean up that mess."

Yanking his arms behind his back, she pushed him to the puddle of beer ahead, where she shoved him to his knees and stood behind him. Slowly, she pushed him forward, with her heel against the back of his head, until his lips were on the floor.

"Clean it with your tongue," she ordered.

Granted, Caleb was a little wary of sipping beer off of a dirty garage floor, but he was too aroused to care and he did as he was told.

Carmen proceeded to kick her shoes off, then she rounded him and stood where he had a perfect view of her feet.

"Get up," she demanded, lifting his chin up with a toe before parting his lips with her foot and shoving it inside his mouth.

Caleb's hard cock sprung out of the open zipper, and it throbbed with every lick. He loved the way she smelled – her natural scent was subtle and it permeated through the girly-scented products she wore. After shoving her entire foot in his mouth all the way against his throat, until he choked on her toes, she slowly drew it out and helped him up.

"Good boy," she praised.

His green eyes leveled with her round tits, and he couldn't keep his gaze off of her erect nipples. Gently, Carmen ran her fingers through his thick brown hair, pulling her strapless dress down with her other hand, freeing one massive tit after the other and shoving his head toward her. He parted his lips, ready to feast on her hard nipples, while enjoying the little groans she let out every time he bit and nibbled.

"That's right, keep going," she moaned, her hand wandering its way to his pants, which she completely pulled down, along with his boxers, before kicking them to a corner. She wrapped her arms around his waist and surprised him with a sudden and firm grip of his ass, her nails digging into his skin.

It was painful, yet pleasurable. He craved more pain, and he was ready to be her obedient whore-boy.

She gave his ass one slap, guiding his head to the other tit, then ran a finger between his cheeks, reaching for his balls. She pushed toward her and lifted up her dress; it was only a piece of fabric around her waist now. He couldn't see her cunt with his face buried between her soft breasts, but he could feel how wet she was on his dick, which was tucked between her juicy pussy lips while her hand caressed his balls.

And just as it felt like he was about to explode, she pulled his head away by the hair and looked down at him with a grin. "Did you just try to fuck me?"

"N-no," he stammered.

Of course, that was a lie. His cock definitely tried to find its way inside her dripping wet pussy.

It seemed that she snorted for a second, but Caleb soon realized that she was hawking a ball of spit, which shortly after, landed on his face. She pulled his hair harder, and he loud out a soft whimper.

"I'm sorry," he said.

"It's going to take a little more effort than that to make it up to me," she scoffed, climbing up the car trunk behind her and spreading her legs wide. Her clit was fat and I could see her pussy leaking from where I was standing. She leaned back and gestured to her pussy with her eyes.

"There's another mess I need you to clean," she commanded. "Quickly, before anyone comes in."

I acquiesced with a nod and wet my lips in anticipation.

For a moment, I froze as I regarded the hottest woman I'd only seen the likes of in porn, sat before me with her legs spread and her clit throbbing for my tongue. I slowly approached her and before I could bend over, she grabbed me by the again, forcing my face against her wet pussy and sliding it around to cover my skin completely in her juices.

I circled my tongue around her clit, and as soon as she spread her lips wider for me, I made sharp flicks with my tongue, watching her squirm and shake her hips. Her deep moans and groans were music to my ears as my tongue made its way to her hole, and my finger caressed her pink little button in circular motion.

Her moans got louder as I slowly pushed my tongue inside her hole, pulling it out before it was halfway inside. She felt tight! And I could feel my cock aching to be inside her as my nose was tucked between her fat lips, completely entrancing me with her scent.

I finally pushed my tongue all the way in, curling it up and back as my finger massaged her clit. She wrapped her legs around my neck and threw her head back, the shaking and twisting of her hips slowly growing to be more vigorous squirming. She finally arched her back and let out a scream before she plopped, completely prostrated on the trunk. Her foot pushed my face away, then she turned on her side and squeezed her thighs together, still softly whimpering.

I waited patiently, my hard cock dripping and ready to be inside her.

Carmen got up, with her hair unkempt, and climbed off the trunk, pulling her dress back in place. She shot me a wide grin, scanning my body from head to toe, then winked.

"You've been good," she praised, reaching for her purse on the trunk. She stuffed her hand inside and pulled out what looked like a gray business card.

"Give me a call sometime," she said, handing me the card and making her way back to the party.

Story 2 - Punishing Drake

"Well, well. Look what we have here," Ada, my wife, said sternly, her voice cutting through the haze. Opening my eyes, my blood chilled at the cold smile on her lips and the devilry in her cerulean blue eyes. The woman in between my legs swiveled her head to see who came in.

She, too, gasped at the coldness in my wife's eyes. The issue wasn't seeing me with another partner. Ada loves to share me with another woman, just as how I love sharing her with other men.

The problem was me getting off without her permission.

My body and my orgasm were under her command. Being my Mistress for five years, she controlled me, and I happily succumbed to her commands. But she'd been gone for two weeks to take care of business, and my teammates urged me to join them for a boy's night out.

And when I say night out, it means going to a club at the nearby town and getting private strip dances at the back room. I was able to resist for a few hours, but with the alcohol warming my insides, the naked photos Ada sent me during my stay in the club, and the suggestive gazes of the women, I became weak to the bone.

It didn't take me long before I was laughing my ass off with my friends and wrapping my arms around two women. A few more drinks and I was lead to a private room where a stunning woman pulled my jeans to my ankles and sucked me off.

You could say I saw stars when I came. It had been too damn long since I finished. I was supposed to tuck this little escapade in the back of my head because I wouldn't want to face the wrath of my Mistress. But when the door opened and revealed my sexy Mistress, my whole body turned into ice. The loud beats that reverberated throughout club weren't enough to quiet down the pounding in my ears. I was fucked and Ada loved it.

You see, I married Ada when we were both eighteen. Fresh out of high school, I asked her traditional parents for her hand in marriage and they quickly welcomed me to the family. It wasn't really an issue considering our families own two of the largest lands in town, and our parents were practically best friends that they may have planned our union since we were babies. I don't mind because Ada was my best friend and my lover. People in our town called us crazy for marrying at a young age but when you find the love of your life, you never want to let go.

Money also wasn't an issue for us because our families were loaded. We both knew we would be owning our family's land and had plans to turn it into a huge business after we graduated from college. So, after marrying, we both got into the same university and moved into a small apartment.

The people around us new Ada was the boss.

She was a sweet five-foot-two red headed beauty with freckles and an alluring smile. I loved her curly red mane of hair, and her smooth, creamy skin. She was petite with a 36B cup and a curvy set of hips. She was a goddess. And often times, I would get told how lucky I was by my baseball teammates to marry such a sexy angel.

I never dared to tell them that she wasn't an angel at all.

I may be over six feet and well-built with a muscular figure, but when Ada sternly looked at me and opened her mouth, I was a goner. She was a Mistress in every sense and I was her sub. Not everyone knew of our power dynamics at home. They might have sensed it, but they always chose to keep their mouths shut. Because Ada may be a sweet angel with a warm sunny smile but when she was in Mistress mode, she was a total boss.

Our power dynamics began when we got married. I knew for a fact that Ada was a dominant woman long before we got married. You can see it in the way she held her head up high and the way she formed her words and thoughts. And Ada knew it, too.

It started with simple orders and gradually evolved until we used bondage and toys. I loved how it became natural for Ada and the thought of her commanding me was deeply arousing. I was used to taking orders, and it was fulfilling for me to serve her. I was a good and obedient sub, but two weeks of celibacy proved to be a challenge for me.

Ada had one rule for me before she left: I wasn't allowed to touch myself.

I thought that was fine initially, but when every night Ada teased me with her sexy phone calls and nude photos, I found it really hard to resist. I took cold showers twice a day to help calm the raging hard on. I was almost successful because Ada told me she'd be back the next day. But I was wrong.

Gulping at my wife's stoic face, I opened and closed my mouth to explain, but no words seemed to come out.

"Leave." Ada ordered the woman between my legs. Sensing my wife's fury, the woman quickly picked up her top and ran out of the room. Once she did so, Ada closed the door with a bang and turned to me. "On your knees and ass in the air."

"Ada..."

"Did I stutter, subbie?" she glared "Ass up."

I knew what she was about to do, and I was embarrassed about the thought of my teammates finding out when I walked out of this room. "No. People might hear us," I begged her.

"You will do what I tell you just like you always do."

"No."

Her cheeks flushed a crimson shade and her eyes raged a storm inside "How dare you argue with me, sub?"

Color drained from my face upon thinking about what I had done.

Fuck. I totally fucked this one up.

"I'm sorry, Mistress. I shouldn't have said that." I somberly hang my head.

"You really shouldn't." she coldly stated. "Now, get on all fours."

Turning my back on her, I did as I was told. My jeans were already undone, so it was easy for her.

"You will take every beating I shall give you, sub."

"Yes, Mistress."

"I will slap you until my hands tire from it. May this be a lesson of obedience for you."

"Yes, Mistress."

Ada wasted no time. Her hands slapped on my ass at a fast rate.

I counted up to twenty, but Ada didn't stop. I was twisting and squirming on the floor as my back stung from the rapid slap of her hands. Biting my lip, my hands lay flat on the cold floor, hoping I could transfer the coldness to my stinging ass. Despite the punishment being given to me, my cock stirred in between my legs.

It took Ada several more slaps before I was sobbing and crying in agony.

"Please, Mistress. I'm sorry," I sobbed to her. "I'm sorry, I will never disobey you again."

"You really shouldn't," she told me, massaging my backside with her hands. Suddenly, she rubbed her thumb along the crack of my ass. Pleasure zoomed through my cock and I could feel it harden. "Hmm, you liked me punishing you, didn't you, you fucking slut?"

"Y-yes." I barely managed to speak.

Her hand slapped my ass again. "I think you haven't learned your lesson yet. It's a good thing I always bring this with me," she said, reaching over to her purse and pulling out a chastity belt.

Looking back at her, her eyes grinned with devilry at the belt in her hands. I gulped as I stared at it.

"You will wear this after I have given you three more beatings," she announced. "You are not allowed to cum without my permission for three weeks. If you fail, I'll add another week. Do you understand?"

"Yes, Mistress."

"Good," she spoke, massaging my burning ass. "Now count to three."

She slapped my ass and I counted, "One."

"Two!"

The final slap made me jerk hard enough for my back to arch. "T-three!"

Crumpling in a heap on the floor, I breathed through my mouth as I tried to get my bearings back. Ada helped me up to put the chastity belt on me. I almost didn't want to put my jeans on because my ass stung so badly, but I had to. I couldn't go out of this room naked. Ass on fire, we walked out of the room with a pleased Mistress by my side.

It was hard to pee with the belt on, but it was harder when I watched my wife shower or dress for the day. Blood would coil at the base of my spine, and

I wouldn't be able to do anything to relieve it. I tried distracting myself from pleasing my wife the past few days. But it was getting harder and harder when she teased me every second of the day.

"Get back on the bed now. On your back, sub!" Ada ordered me. Wanting to please her, I quickly crawled to bed wearing my white shower robe. We were supposed to be attending a party hosted by our family's friend downtown, when an idea sparked in Ada's mind.

"Hands on the headboard." She ordered and I did so. "Good boy."

I glowed at her response. Eyes flashing in devilry, she hooked her black satin dress up to her waist. My eyes gaped at her naked ass and pussy.

Crawling on top of me, she straddled her pussy on my face

"Fuck me with your tongue, sub. Make me come!"

Pleased to worship my Mistress, she lowered herself, and I flicked my tongue against her cunt, licking her sweet juices. A contented sigh fell on her lips, and she lowered herself even more for more pressure. Licking every inch of her pussy, my tongue lapped at her scent and juices. I swirled my tongue in between her folds and sucked on her tiny oversensitive clit. Her breathes came out in gasps as I licked the opening of her pussy and flicked my tongue inside. She moaned and began rocking her hips on my face. Digging my tongue inside of her, her movements became frantic and the bulge in my cock grew to life.

I wanted nothing more than to bury myself in her sweet pussy.

I probably wouldn't last long once I sheathed inside of her. With that image in my mind, I fucked her fast and deeply, wanting to make her come. Alternating between the inside of her pussy and her clit, I buried myself in her and I felt her shake violently on top of me. Her back arched in response and her head fell back as a cry escaped from her lips.

My cock was hard inside the confines of my chastity belt.

Opening her eyes, a slow sensual grin was on her lips before she bent down and kissed me on the lips. She tasted her scent on my tongue and I glorified at the way her hands ran along my arms.

Pulling back, she softly said "You've been a really good sub these past few weeks. Let's put it to the test tonight."

Frowning at her words, she wickedly smiled before climbing out of bed and pulling me up. "Come on Drake. We don't want to be late to the party."

Still confused at her words, I gussied up before putting on my suit and tie as I watched Ava applied her makeup. The same Cheshire grin was on her face when I held my arm out to her. Whatever her plans were going be, I was sure in for a treat.

I was about to find out about it when our host Peter, a man who was twice our age, greeted us. He had a friendly smile and a well-built body. He had a room under control like an experienced domme in a room full of subs. As he conversed with my wife in front of me, I noticed his hand surreptitiously stroking her arms, hips, and legs.

I had a hint of where this would be headed. My suspicions were confirmed when Peter invited us to his home.

"Ada informed me of your punishment," Peter not-so-subtly said once we reached his room. Ada grinned and patted my arm in comfort.

"Let's put to the test how much you can resist coming, sub." Ada grinned at me. "Today is your last day. If you can stop yourself from coming until midnight, your punishment is over. If not, I'll add another week to your punishment, while Peter fucks me in front of you."

"Will this please you, Mistress?" I asked her.

"Yes, it will." She nodded her head.

"Then I will do it."

She grinned and began kissing me passionately. My response pleased her greatly and my chest heaved in appreciation. Ada ran her hand along my arms, my chest and my pants. She pulled the coat off of my arms and began unbuttoning my shirt. "Undress me, sub."

I unzipped the back of her dress as she removed my shirt and pants. I wasn't wearing anything underneath. Pushing me to the chair, Peter handed her cuffs and chained both of my hands to the chair.

Kissing me on the lips, she whispered. "Don't cum."

"I won't, Mistress," I raggedly replied, despite my desires.

"Good." She grinned and joined Peter on the bed, who was naked, too. "You can only watch. But you cannot come. Not without my permission."

"Yes, Mistress."

Turning her attention to Peter, I watched them kiss and run their hands over each other. My balls tightened as I watched Peter suck and nibble at Ada's huge tits. I loved Ada's tits but I loved her tight pussy even more. And Peter seemed to enjoy it, too, as he slipped a finger inside Ava's moist heat and began finger fucking her. With Ada on top, she let out a gasp as she held on to Peter's shoulders. Her hips rocked to the rhythm of the finger inside of her. The motion of his fingers began to grow frantic and Ada's hand cupped his erect cock.

My cock jerked inside the chastity belt and I hissed a breath, desperate for her touch, too. Sensing my gaze, Peter and Ada grinned before they changed positions. Ada's ass was in the air while Peter lined his cock along her entrance. I gulped as I watched him run the tip of his cock from Ada's clit to her sweet pussy lips. I groaned when he slowly thrust himself inside her pussy.

My hands gripped the arms of the chair as Peter roughly moved in and out of Ada's pussy. The sound of his balls slapping onto her dripping wet cunt, and Ada's breathy moans were making me crazy. My cock throbbed inside of my pants and I desperately prayed for the clock to turn to twelve.

I wanted to come, to sink my dick inside her pussy more than anything. Peter's movements began to grow frantic as Ada's moans grew breathier and louder. I knew, for a fact, that they were close to climaxing. I had to hold my breath as I watched them fall apart in a cacophony of groans and moans.

I thought, perhaps, they would stop, but they continued to fuck each other until I was begging Ada to release me.

"You want to cum, slave?" Ada teased, fingering her come-covered pussy.

"Yes, Mistress. Please, please, make me come," I begged her, tears in my eyes. My cock was painfully hard and purple.

"Fuck my pussy with your tongue until midnight," she said. "Release him, Peter."

Like an obedient man, Peter removed my restraints and I rushed to her, kneeling in between her legs and began devouring her wet pussy. The taste of her come and Peter's was so delicious that it intensified my desire.

"Hands on your back, sub," she commanded "You're not allowed to touch me yet."

"Yes, mistress." I obediently nodded and began worshipping her. I was close to rubbing my cock on the sheets. It didn't help that Peter was sucking Ada's tits.

Fuck!

"You can't come yet, Drake," she warned me as I let out a moan when Peter caressed my hair. My overly sensitive skin was about to explode into a million pieces.

Tightening my arms on my back, I focused on making *her* come. She was so close that when the clock chimed to midnight, everyone froze in surprise. Looking up, Ada grinned before pulling me on the bed and tying my arms on either side of bed post.

Taking the key out, she released my chastity belt, and hovered over my engorged cock. Peter walked to my side and pushed his dick on my lips. "Suck Peter's cock. Make him come, and I'll make you come. You are not allowed to finish until I say so."

"Yes, Mistress."

Opening my mouth, Peter's nine-inch cock choked me to the hilt. I moaned as Ada's sweet lips wrapped around my cock. My whole body froze when Ada began to move her sweet hands and plump lips up and down the length of my dick.

Fuck! Fuck!

My hips jerked in response, making me hit the back of Ada's throat.

Fuck! I must resist!

Focusing on the cock in my mouth, I sucked Peter until his dick leaked inside my mouth. Ada's hands moved rigorously on my dick, her thumb brushing over the rim.

My balls tightened, and the familiar ache in my bones was back. I was so close. So fucking close. Swallowing every inch of Peter's cum, I pulled away from him with a pop and begged for my Mistress to let me come.

"Please, Mistress. May I please come? I'm so close," I begged her. "Please, oh fuck, please," I moaned.

Grinning wickedly, my insides flushed when she straddled me and positioned the head of my cock along her entrance. With eyes wide open, I watched as she slowly shoved my rock-hard dick inside of her, wrapping me with her velvet and moist heat. When my cock filled her to the tilt, we both groaned in unison.

"Mistress," I sobbed, my balls as tight as they can be. "Please."

"Hush, slave. You can take more," she commanded, moving up and down. "Do not come."

"Y-yes, mistress," I choked out, sobbing in her chest as she held me in her arms. Wrapping her arms around me, she moved up and down, fast and hard. I was so delirious and shaking with need that by the time Ada said granted me permission to come, I was losing it.

Screaming and arching my back for the release I so badly wanted, I was halfway through when Peter called out, still sitting beside me. "That's enough," he said with a grin.

Ada let out a sinister chuckle, quickly pulling herself away and watching me squirm beneath her.

"You did well, slave," she said proudly. "Maybe next time, I'll let you finish."

Story 3 - Like a Dream

I always looked forward to nine p.m. when my mistress would come online and to video chat. She was a goddess demanding to be worshiped that punished me when I failed to satisfy her. It made me hard just thinking about it.

I refrained from touching my quickly stiffening cock, though. She hadn't let me cum in a week and it was pure torture to touch myself at this point. My balls ached, the head of my cock dripped precum, and I had a hard time focusing on anything else.

Sitting on the couch, I leaned my head back and stared at the ceiling, just imagining my mistress's touch on my cock. I pulsed, my swollen member rubbing against my jeans.

There was a knock at the door and I jumped up, startled.

"Who is it?" I called suspiciously, walking towards the door. It was hard to walk with my cock pressed so firmly against my jeans, but I managed to reach the door with only a few soft moans escaping.

There was no answer. Just another knock.

I shook my head and yanked the door open to find myself face-to-face with the most glorious pair of breasts I had ever seen. They were pushed up and spilling from a seductive low-cut shirt, her nipples hard and pressing against the fabric. I swallowed hard and looked up to my mistress.

"What..?" I murmured, my eyes going wide.

"Well, aren't you going to invite me in, slut?" she purred, her breasts bouncing with her laughter.

"You...how did you...?" I tried to find my words.

"How did I find you? It's a secret," her red lips smirked at me. "Now, may I come in?"

I paused, my stalker senses tingling, but the way she looked at me made my already hard cock ooze a little more precum. The front of my jeans had a small wet spot on them now, and I started flushing as she looked down and noticed.

"Have you been touching yourself?" she frowned.

"No! No, ma'am." I was quick to reply.

"Good. I had you saving all that delicious cum for the party tonight."

"Party?" I asked weakly.

"The one I keep in this bag," she gestured at the large black bag I hadn't noticed sitting next to her. It was her toy bag, the one she used to tease me online.

My head warned me not to let her in, but my cock throbbed at the thought of her using me like she had promised.

"Can I carry your bag?" I gave in.

"Good boy. Yes, you may," she sauntered in with a fantastic sway of her hips, her high heels clicking on the hardwood floor. Her skirt was so short I could see the curve of her ass just below the hem. I swallowed hard and followed her inside with the bag.

"What a wonderful apartment," she turned to face me. "Strip."

I hesitated for only a moment before struggling quickly out of my clothes, leaving them in a pile on the floor beside me. I stood naked before her and couldn't help but blush as she walked a circle around me, studying me from every side.

She stopped in front of me and smiled down at my hard cock. "Does it ache, slut?"

"Yes, Mistress," I said softly.

"And do your balls?"

"Y-yes, Mistress."

"Good. Get on your knees."

I dropped to the ground and watched as she opened her toy bag and pulled out a riding crop. My cock throbbed at the thought of her using it on me and my balls tightened against my body.

She turned and frowned at me. "Spread your legs wider. I want your cock presented to me at all times. It is no longer your cock. It is mine. Am I clear?"

"Yes, Mistress," I whimpered, widening my knees so that my hard cock pointed at her.

"Good boy," she purred, approaching me and smiling.

She gently raised my cock with the tip of the riding crop then, with a flick of her wrist, flipped it down on the head. I let out a shriek while tears came to my eyes and my cock throbbed from both pain and need.

"Now, now. We can't be having that sort of noise, can we?" She reached into the bag and brought out a penis-shaped gag, gently pressing it into my mouth and fastening it behind my head. "Where were we? Oh, yes."

The flick of the crop landed on my balls this time, and I jumped, shrieking into the gag. The long latex cock in my throat muffled the sound and all that came out was a whimper.

My mistress smiled wickedly at me, then began popping my balls and cock with the riding crop over and over as I tried to beg for mercy through the gag. The pain was intense, but I could feel the pleasure beginning to warm up in my stomach. I started thrusting my hips toward her to meet the sting of the crop.

She stopped suddenly. "Are you going to cum from being beaten?" she asked in surprise.

I made an affirmative noise through the gag as I gasped for breath.

"What a pain slut," she smiled viciously at me. My cock and balls ached immensely and I was shaking with need as she rummaged through her toy bag again. She produced a large wooden paddle with a heart burned into it and waved it in front of me. "On all fours. Present your ass."

I achingly flipped over and realized my arms and legs were shaking. It was hard to hold myself up, but I knew I couldn't let my mistress down and braced myself accordingly.

"Crawl," she hissed. I paused for a moment in confusion, but with a massive swing, she landed a resounding blow on my ass. "I said crawl!"

I whimpered through the gag and began slowly making my way around the room as she landed blow after blow on my reddening ass. My cock was dripping precum on the floor, and she laughed as I crawled a circle through it. Tears streamed down my face from the pain and humiliation.

With a final resounding blow, she landed the hardest strike yet, and I collapsed on the floor, writhing in agony. My cock was throbbing so hard that I was afraid I would explode and she stood over me, laughing.

"You're a disgusting slut. Do you know what that gets you?" she smirked. "Fucked in the ass."

I lay on the floor trembling, my need making me light-headed, pain throbbing through my body. She grabbed a massive double-sided strap-on from her bag and pulled her skirt up to reveal that she was wearing no panties.

"I'm going to cum while fucking you in the ass, and you are not to cum at all. Is that clear?" she pressed one side of the strap-on into her wet pussy and moaned slightly. "In fact, I'm going to cum twice while fucking you in the ass, and you are going to let me do it because you're a slut, and you are mine to use. Is that clear?"

I moaned around the gag and got to my knees slowly. My arms and legs were shaking so hard that I couldn't hold myself up anymore and collapsed back to the floor.

"Oh, dear. Looks like it's time to head into the bedroom. Crawl the way, slut." Her smile was sinister.

Shaking, I began making my way on my hands and knees into the bedroom where I collapsed on my bed from the waist up. I turned to look at her and watched as she covered the strap-on in lube before kneeling behind me and gently fingering my hole.

"Remember, you're not to cum," she said as she pressed one finger deep inside me. I writhed against her hand and moaned. She gently began rubbing against my prostate and I whimpered as my cock throbbed and pulsed. I was so close to the edge, but I tried to hold myself back for her. She slowly pulled her finger out and pressed the head of the dildo against me.

"Relax, this is very big," her voice held a smirk.

The massive head of the strap-on pierced me, and I tensed up, tightening around it. She whispered soothing things and I relaxed again, feeling the smooth silicone enter me, filling me, making me throb inside and out.

Then she turned on the vibrator.

I squealed against the gag and writhed as the vibrations hit against my prostate, my cock oozing precum that dripped onto the floor. I could barely hold myself back from cumming. I was getting close – so close – and then it all stopped.

"I know you almost came," she whispered in my ear. "Don't do it."

I whimpered damply around the gag and she laughed. The vibrator was turned back on and she moaned as she began to smoothly slide in and out of me. Her hand reached around me and grabbed my balls painfully, squeezing and rolling them in her palm. It was easier not to think about cumming when my balls were being tormented.

"I'm going to cum," she said breathlessly, beginning to pound the dildo into me. Her hand clutched my balls so hard I almost screamed, and I choked on the cock gag in my mouth. I couldn't help slamming back against her to meet the thrusts, driving the strap-on deeper into me with each movement.

She cried out, and I felt her body spasm against my back. It was almost my undoing but she squeezed my balls again painfully, and I pressed back against the strap-on in surrender.

"You...you slut," she panted, "You made me cum too fast. Your ass is just perfect for fucking. Stay right here."

I heard her get up and walk back to the living room, then the sound of her bag hitting the floor behind me made me jerk. She dug through it for a moment before she passed a large silver butt plug before my eyes. "This is for you, slut. It'll hold my place for me."

She pressed the tip against my hole and slowly, ever so slowly, slid it into me. It was large, almost as big as the strap-on had been, and I moaned as it filled me, my asshole closing around the base.

"Good boy. Now you're going to clean me up." She undid the strap on the gag and sat on the edge of the bed with her legs spread. "Lick."

My sore mouth formed a delighted smile as I buried my face between her legs. Her smooth pussy tasted like heaven, the scent of her tickling my nostrils as I cleaned all the wetness from between her thighs. She pressed one high heel against my cock and I froze, feeling the sharp heel positioned against the slit.

"Did I tell you to stop?" she growled.

"No, Mistress." I lapped at her pussy, sucking gently on her clit.

She leaned her head back and closed her eyes as she gently ground her shoe into my cock. I could feel the heel beginning to enter me and I moaned as she pushed my head harder into her pussy.

"I'm going to cum again," she breathed harder. "Keep going!"

I licked faster, my cock throbbing against her shoe, grinding itself into the heel that was dangerously close to entering me. Her thighs shook around my head and then she was squeezing me between them so tightly I could barely breathe. I never stopped sucking and licking, though, intent on her pleasure splashing across my face.

"You fucking slut. Look at the mess you made," she gasped as she came down from her orgasm. "Lick the floor clean."

I backed away and began to lick our combined juices, her sweet orgasm and my salty precum. Together, they were a heady potion and I felt my cock, which was still so hard, begging to be touched while my asshole throbbed, the butt plug a reminder that she could fuck my ass whenever she wanted. I was overwhelmed.

I sat back on my heels, knees spread, and looked up at her in a haze of pain and pleasure. She truly was a goddess.

"Get on the bed, face up." She stood and leaned into the toy bag, pulling a small leather pouch from its depths.

I obeyed instantly and lay on the bed, my cock standing straight up at attention. It throbbed in sync with my heartbeat and she watched it for a moment and laughed.

"Get ready," she purred, opening the pouch beside me. Inside it were metal rods, some smooth, some textured, some hollow, and I felt my mouth go dry. Sounding rods. She was going to sound me.

She pulled a small smooth rod from the pouch and held it in front of my face. "Let's start small, shall we?"

She balanced the rod at the very tip of my cock, with one finger holding my shaft steady, then slowly began to enter me. I moaned quietly, the pain crackling through my body before instantly changed to pleasure. I wanted more.

"Is this not enough for you?" she asked, seeming to read my mind.

"No, Mistress," I managed to breathe out.

"Good. Let's get something more fun in there." She placed the small rod aside and grabbed a large textured one. It looked like metal balls chained together, and I wriggled in anticipation.

With a steady hand, she placed the first ball against the slit in my cock and smiled at me, never breaking eye contact as she pressed each ridge into my aching member. I moaned and pressed up against the rod, forcing it deeper. Precum spilled around the rod, dripping down my cock, tickling my balls.

"Mistress..." I whimpered, pleasure blossoming inside me from so many different places. My ass still hurt from the paddling, but now it just added to the growing warmth in my belly. I needed to cum so badly that I could hardly stand it.

"Time for another nice ass fucking, you slut," she said brightly, leaving the rod deep in my cock. The rod was so heavy, it pulled my cock down to rest on my balls and it was all I could do to stop myself from stroking myself.

She pulled the massive strap-on back onto the bed and adjusted it into her pussy, pulling the large buttplug out of me and placing it aside. My asshole gaped and begged to be filled again.

"You are a dirty little slut, aren't you?" she asked.

"Yes, Mistress," I whispered.

"Say it," she demanded.

"I'm...I'm a dirty little slut," my voice was quiet, unsteady.

"Good," she took a small bottle of lube with a spout on top and pressed it into my aching hole. With a firm squeeze, she poured cool lube into me and I thrust my hips up in pleasure.

She placed the head of the strap-on against my asshole and then suddenly slammed it home. I screamed out in surprise, my hands quickly covering my mouth as she viciously pounded me over and over. My cock slammed back and forth, the rod in it making it hit my balls painfully with every thrust.

"Tell me how much you like this," she hissed.

"Mistress, I love it!" I yelped.

"Love what?"

"I love being fucked in the ass! I'm a little slut and I love being ass fucked! Please, don't stop fucking me!" I couldn't help myself; I was so close to losing control. I felt so dirty and slutty, and I loved hearing myself say it.

"Doesn't your cock love the attention, too?" she laughed, pulling and pushing the rod inside me. My balls tightened against my body and I moaned loudly.

"Mistress, may I cum?" I begged.

"No. I'm not done with you yet. I still need to cum again, remember?" she chided.

I groaned and writhed with the rhythm of her fucking my ass and my cock. My body felt so full, and I was losing myself to the feeling.

With a pop, she pulled the sounding rod out of me and pressed a new one into the slit. This one was hollow and rounded and felt amazing as it cooled my hot cock.

Then she turned on the strap-on's vibrator.

My ass spasmed, and I thrust up against her hand, almost cumming immediately. "Mistress!" I cried out.

"Do you like getting fucked like this, slut?" she growled.

"Yes, Mistress! Please use my holes for your pleasure! My cock is yours! My ass is yours! Please use my body to cum!" I could hear myself babbling, but I couldn't seem to stop. I was a dirty slut and we both knew it.

"Mmm, I like that. What a good fuck toy," she rolled her hips and the head of the strap-on brushed against my prostate. I cried out, my hips trying to force the thick silicone deeper inside me. "I'm close. When I cum, you may cum," she said, her breathing growing labored.

"Thank you, Mistress!" I exclaimed in relief. Part of me hoped that she'd come soon, but another part hoped she never came so I could be her little fuck toy forever.

"Ah, good boy. Just a little longer..." she rubbed a hand over her nipples and moaned as her head fell back. Her hips beat a rhythm into my ass and it was all I could do to hang on and not cum.

"Mistress..." I begged, "I can't...I can't wait..."

"You will wait...for me..." she panted. Her rhythm grew erratic, and then she cried out, her body stiffening as she began to pound me in earnest, the head of the strap-on mercilessly beating into my prostate. With both hands, she pointed my cock at my face and I looked down the hollow tube into my cock, suddenly realizing I was going to cum on my own face.

"No, Mistress, no!" I cried out as my body spasmed, my cum shooting through the tube and onto my face. It was a violent orgasm, hot pleasure shooting out of me, my mouth open in a shriek. I tasted my own cum as she adjusted my cock to better target my mouth. It was an eternity of pleasure, and she began to stroke my cock to release all of the cum I had been saving for a week. My face and chest were covered in hot juices, and it leaked from between my lips as I attempted to swallow through heaving gasps.

"Dirty slut." She smiled down at me, then pulled both the sounding rod and strap-on out. I lay weakly on the bed, my eyes shutting of their own volition, as she walked between the bedroom and bathroom, cleaning her toys and repacking her bag.

"Get some rest. I'll see myself out." I could hear the smile in her voice as I drifted off to sleep.

The morning sunshine brought me back to consciousness, and I rolled over sorely. My entire body ached, from my ass to my cock to my mouth, and I blinked up at the ceiling.

I gingerly got out of bed and headed to my computer. I scrolled through my friend's list but didn't see my mistress's name. I attempted to search for her, but no profiles matched my search.

She was just gone. Just like a dream.

Story 4 - Diary Entry

Today was a good day.

The wife and I went shopping and she had me wearing my new chastity belt under my pants. It was a cold stainless-steel contraption with a massive hook for my asshole and a urethral sound for my cock. I could barely walk with everything in place and I kept trying to get hard knowing that it was locked up tight around my cock and there was no way I could get out of it. The wife wore the key around her neck on a chain and smiled at me as she asked me to bend over and grab things from the bottom shelves.

She kept telling me to lift with my knees, knowing full well that I would feel the hook in my ass harder if I did it. But I obeyed. She told me the faces I was making were adorable as she played with the key and it made me blush. I love when she says I'm adorable.

As we were checking out she said she forgot the soap and told me to run to get it. I knew she meant run, too. Trying to run with a hook in my ass and a tube in my cock was torture of the most amazing kind. It was more like a waddling run but I made good time to the back of the store and found the soap. I ran/waddled back up front just in time to throw the soap on the belt and she graced me with the most amazing smile. I felt my heart do a flip. Her smile could light up the biggest room and I felt my cock trying to harden again and meeting the steel of the cage around it. This belt was truly amazing and she was amazing for getting it for me.

We checked out and walked back to the car and she had me load all the groceries into the trunk and return the cart. I was excited to get home so I was quick about it.

When I slid into the car, gingerly, she told me we were going the long way home. I begged for her to reconsider because the long way home is on gravel roads and I knew it would be torture to drive across that with the chastity belt on, but she just laughed and told me to hang on.

It wasn't so bad to start with as the gravel road was pretty well worn. But then we came to the uneven, bumpy, torture road, and I couldn't help but moan out loud as every bounce and jolt rammed the hook inside me a little more. My cock vibrated against the steel cage and I kept getting partially hard, hitting the cage, and softening, over and over. I couldn't help myself, I started begging for her to have mercy, to take us home, to make it stop, but she just pulled a U-turn and took us back across the most unforgiving parts of the road.

She said she'd forgotten something at the store and we absolutely had to go back for it. I groaned and then squealed as we hit a really massive dip. My asshole was tingling and I couldn't wait to get home and beg for her to fuck me.

We pulled into the parking lot and we walked, well, she walked, I limped, back into the store. She led me towards the clothing section and I groaned internally. I knew she liked to browse the clothes, and it would take a while. When she turned a frown on me I realized that I had actually let the groan out loud. I felt like I paled and blushed at the same time and my stomach did a flip.

With a smirk she picked out a very small pink dress and led me towards the fitting rooms. I squirmed inside because I knew it was for me. I was both incredibly excited and extremely embarrassed.

She told me to change into it and come out to show her. I said, 'yes, wife' and did as I was told. I was only wearing a shirt and jeans, no underwear, and the skirt barely covered my cock. I could see the metal of the chastity belt if I moved too fast.

I called out to her that it didn't fit right and she demanded to see. With a deep breath I primly walked out of the fitting room and faced her, my face bright red, pulling the skirt down to remain modest.

She smiled in delight and told me how cute I looked. Then she demanded that I release the skirt and let her see how it flowed. I hesitated, looking left and right before I slowly released the skirt. I knew it lifted slightly and my chastity belt was visible as she laughed that it was exactly the right length.

My cock tried to harden in the cage as I blushed harder. She walked a circle around me, then lifted the front of the dress and smiled at me. I could have died from embarrassment and horniness at the same time as she tapped on the cage encircling my cock. She asked if I liked the dress and I could barely speak. I was so scared someone would see us that I felt light headed.

She pulled me in for a kiss and I felt her nip at my lips as she pulled gently on the chastity belt. It moved inside me and I groaned into her mouth. She knows how much of a little whore I am for humiliation and she uses me so well.

The kiss ended too soon and she spun me around and smacked my ass as she told me to get dressed again. I was relieved but kind of wanted to keep the dress on. I always liked the way I looked in a short skirt.

I shuffled back to the changing room and got dressed again while admiring the way the steel of the chastity glowed against my skin. I looked like an owned slut and I started to get hard again before the cage blocked me; it made me smile.

We started towards the front of the store when I suddenly knew I had to use the bathroom. I asked very politely if I could be relieved and she said no. Okay, I can hold it until we get home. We checked out again and headed back towards the car where she took a right towards the gravel road.

I groaned in protest and she laughed at me, telling me how good I had been and that she was entitled to a little fun. I braced myself for the bumps but it was all I could do to hold on to the door as every jostle and jolt vibrated inside me. My cock rattled against the cage and the tube inside me caused me to clench up trying not to pee on myself.

I begged for her to take us home as I crossed and uncrossed my legs but I couldn't even clutch at myself through the steel. I was terrified that I would piss in the car!

She granted me mercy and we finally pulled into our driveway. She ordered me to bring in the groceries and I begged to be allowed to use the bathroom first, but she shook her head. She said that there were refrigerated items and I had to get them all put away first. I could feel myself shuddering from the need to pee and I started running between the house and the car as fast as the belt would let me.

I admit I didn't put the groceries away with the care that I normally do; things were crooked and out of place, the fridge was stuffed instead of organized. The wife watched all this from the doorway and frowned. She said that until the kitchen was the way it was supposed to be I was not allowed to relieve myself.

Tears pricked at my eyes and I began to neatly organize everything. It was torture squatting and standing over and over but it helped me to hold it in. I almost peed on myself when I squatted in front of the fridge and the cold air washed over me, but I managed to hold on through strength of will alone.

The kitchen was done and organized and perfect within ten minutes and I couldn't stop dancing around as I begged to use the bathroom yet again. The wife smiled and told me to strip down and I immediately obeyed. I stood before her in nothing but the chastity belt and whimpered softly.

She finally relented and slowly unlocked the cage. She pulled the hook from my ass and the tube from my cock gently then ushered me into the bathroom. I was nearly crying as I asked for permission to use the toilet. She paused and watched me dance back and forth then smiled and said I was allowed.

I have never been so relieved in my life and I moaned in pleasure as I peed for what seemed like ages. The wife stood at the door and watched me with a pleased smile, congratulating me on holding it in for so long. I felt pride rise inside me and wriggled in happiness that she was happy with me. I finished up and knelt on the tile before her, thanking her for the use of the toilet and for training me to be a better husband.

She patted me on the head and told me to put on the dress we had just bought. I felt a delighted glow light up my face and curled my toes in anticipation. The dress really was adorable and I now had my cock free hanging down below the hem of the skirt.

With a practiced hand she flicked the head of my cock and I jumped and began to grow hard. She knew how much I liked having my cock tormented under a dress and I couldn't hide the smile growing on my face.

She pulled the evil stick out of her toy bag and told me to start cleaning. We did this once a week, where I dusted and vacuumed and swept and mopped and did general household tasks as she followed me around and punished my cock and balls when I raised my arms too high. It was my favorite part of the week.

I always start dusting on the highest shelves and the swish and thwack of the evil stick on my cock is a wonderful reminder that she expects the utmost care when I'm cleaning. I keep my arms raised so that she can see how hard I'm getting even though the evil stick is tormenting my balls now and it's getting harder to dust the shelves.

I finish the top shelves, quickly get through the middle ones, then move on to the bottom shelves where I have to kneel and sometimes crawl to get every corner clean. The wife whips my ass as I crawl across the floor between shelves and I yelp and whimper after every hit. I want more on my cock and balls and I know exactly how to ask for it.

I pause after finishing the last shelf, then raise my ass in the air with my legs spread so she can see my balls and cock, so hard, hanging between my legs. I beg for a hit and am startled when I feel her hand tickling my balls instead of the evil stick punishing me. I giggle and squirm and almost collapse as her fingernails scrape against my most sensitive parts.

She tells me again how good I've been today and how proud she is of me, then with a massive swing the evil stick embeds itself between my balls. I howl in pain and collapse to the floor, my stomach twisting with nausea. I ask if I may have another as I shakily get back to my hands and knees and she obliges, this time hitting my shaft. I squeal like a little pig and shuffle forward a few steps. I thank her and she pats my head and tells me she wants to play a game.

I am so excited immediately and watch as she pulls out my favorite vibrating prostate plug. She tells me to bend over and lubes up the toy before inserting it inside me, then explains the rules. I am to sweep, mop, and vacuum the whole house without cumming.

She knows this will be a challenge for me as she has trained me very well to cum from a prostate massage.

I pull out the broom and begin sweeping as she turns on the vibrator on the lowest setting, then, as I begin to sweep, she switches it to high immediately. I cry out and drop to my knees, my cock immediately weeping precum and I can barely hold back the orgasm that threatens me. She reminds me that I'm not allowed to cum and switches the vibrator to a high-low-high setting.

This is my favorite setting and I roll onto my back on the floor and begin to pump my hips helplessly. I can't stand and can't stop and it's a shock as the evil stick begins to beat my cock and balls relentlessly. I beg for release and the wife says no, get up and sweep. I try to turn over, to crawl my way to the broom, but it's useless and I roll onto my back once again.

I cry out that I'm going to cum and I can't stop it and the wife, with infinite mercy, grants my wish and demands I cum for her. And that's all it takes. My cock exploded, shooting cum to the ceiling and coming down to splatter on me. The orgasm was so visceral that I screamed over and over and finally started to come down as the vibrator slowly switched lower, then off.

The wife asked if I was ready to sweep now and I laughed as she sat next to me and began to stroke my head. My body was still trembling and I curled up around her and breathed in her scent. She is the light of my life and I couldn't make it without her and I will do whatever it takes to make her happy.

She told me how good I had been and that she had asked me to do something unfair and she was sorry. I snuggled closer to her and told her that I would do anything for her, including lick up my cum if she wanted. She paused and I curled my toes in anticipation but she laughed and said that I hadn't mopped yet and didn't want me to lick the dirty floor. She's always looking out for me.

Yeah, today was a good day.

Story 5 - The Reeling

I'm a woman with an unusual desire.

The sort of desire that's only whispered about. You see, I love being pleased by a man, but not just any man; the unconventional man with the gut to submit to me...utterly and irrevocably. And I have found many ways to reel them in.

I go on this little hunting adventure I call *The Reeling*. It's a bit like fishing, actually.

The mall is the easiest place with a lot of fish, but it's not my favorite. See, I like to have fun while I hunt and, the more challenge the hunt scene provides, the more excitement and anticipation runs through my blood.

Everywhere I went, I dressed to command the attention of the male, and for this particular adventure, I wore a pantsuit. I did not need to reveal much to clue them in on my intent. Tapered pants sheathed my legs, paired with a jacket cut to fit every contour of my torso. I wore no blouse underneath the jacket so it revealed just enough cleavage to distract the man.

It didn't take long to spot a potential target, a man throwing a coin into the fountain. He seemed generous enough to part with his money, and a generous man made a good lover. But it was a wishing fountain, meaning he could also be desperate enough for his wish to come true. Either way, I knew I could use him to my advantage and there was only one way to find out if he was up to the challenge.

I scanned his hands for a ring. There was none. Good. I never went for married men. After throwing three coins into the fountain, he moved away and sat on a bench nearby. That was my cue. I walked up to him, my strides confident and my gaze locked on his face. His eyes visibly widened in surprise when he saw me walking straight to him, and when I sat on the empty spot beside him, he was confused.

I introduced myself, giving him a name that was not really mine—a tactic to avoid needy men. We talked for a bit. His name was Derek, worked in Tech, lived alone with his dog, and there was no mention of a woman. He was well-dressed in a black t-shirt and a pair of jeans that clung to powerfully built legs with a grey jacket to top it off. He was very good-looking, but the way he leaned close, and the unconcealed lust in his eyes, spoke volumes of his loneliness.

He will do.

I cut our conversation short and slipped a folded card into his hands. The card had a phone number and an address on one side, and requirements to submit to me sexually on the other. I always made sure that my men knew what they were getting into before pressing that dial button. With a soft, lingering kiss on his cheek, I stood and walked away. I could feel his eyes on my ass as I walked.

He called.

Three hours after meeting at the mall, he called, asking when he could see me. I was free that night, so I gave him the green-light. He had a small duffle bag with him when he arrived, and I must admit, I was quite surprised at the contents of the bag: a crop, massage oil, and leather restraints. I had the same tools, of course – all except massage oil, which gave me an idea.

We didn't waste any time getting down to business. I asked him to strip, and he did eagerly. I bent him over, parted his butt cheeks—causing him to shiver—and inserted a lubricated plug into his ass. His erection swelled even more when he straightened. I so loved when a man's cock swelled with a plug inside him. I then shackled his ankles with the leather ankle restraint he'd brought, leaving just enough space for him to walk awkwardly...well, it was more of a waddle than a walk.

I lay on the tiled floor of the room that I dedicated for my pleasure, and commanded him to take my blue chiffon dress off with his teeth. They grazed my skin as he pulled my dress, causing my nipples to tingle and my pussy to flow.

When I was completely naked, I asked him to rub the massage oil all over my body and massage every inch of me. Oh, Derek was good with his hands. He massaged my slippery skin, kneading and caressing, making me moan with pleasure. When he reached my breasts, he first massaged each one with both hands, taking care to twist the nipples and flick them with his fingers, then dedicated one hand to each breast and kneaded them at the same time.

By now, my pussy was aching to be touched and I parted my legs for him. I could see when his engorged penis did a little leap. It was that excited. He drizzled some oil onto my pussy. It was cold. Combine that with the warmth of his hands, and the sensation was blindingly arousing. His fingers ran circles around my throbbing clit as his other hand stroked my labia.

"Stick your finger in," I ordered, trying to control my breathing.

He inserted a finger into my slick pussy, then another one followed. He curled both fingers slightly inwards and began moving them, stroking that hidden spot deep inside me. My pleasure mounted, and I lifted my face up to his for a kiss. We kissed passionately, tongues tangling, and lips sucking on one another. Seeing how the kiss distracted him from working my pussy, I decided I had a better use for his lips. I pushed his head down and directed him to my pussy where he began lapping like a hungry puppy.

His tongue ran up and down my clit, then in and out my pussy. The more pussy juice he licked off, the more I made. My ecstasy built until I could feel nothing but the sensation in my body. I cried out, clutching his head. He tried to move, but I restrained him, and made him continue. There was an even more intense pleasure that came after the first wave of my orgasm had crashed, and my whole body shook with it.

Derek's face was drenched when he came up. "What do you want me to do next?" He asked, clearly eager to please me.

I was still weak from my orgasm, so I asked him to clean me up. He fetched a towel and filled a bowl with warm water before settling to begin cleaning me up. He was careful and meticulous. After cleaning my body, he cleaned the floor while I made myself comfortable on the bed.

His cock did not go flaccid one bit while he mopped the floor, if anything, it appeared to have gone more rigid. Perhaps it was time I rewarded him. After all, he'd done all I'd asked and more.

"Come here," I said.

He walked to the bed, his member dancing provocatively with every step. A smile curved my lips. He was beautiful...I thought about keeping him a while. He was definitely spending the night here, that was for sure. Reaching behind him, I removed the plug stuffing his ass and flung it to the side, then settled back down and parted my legs wide.

"Now, take your cock in hand and press it to my clit," I instructed.

Derek did as he was told. His face had that stupidly adorable look; a cross between sleepy, sheepish and happy. Taking his hard erection in hand, he pressed the wet tip to my clit and held it there, waiting for his next order. I took my sweet time and enjoyed the play of emotions on his face.

It was the sweetest form of torture for him. His jaw was clenched as he made himself hold back. Beads of sweat covered his forehead, and his eyes were unfocused. I'll bet he was pleading with me in his mind to let him have some release.

"Mmmm," I moaned, then moved my hips in circles around his leaking cock. "Move with me. Make me cum, but don't you dare let yourself come."

He shut his eyes very briefly, ostensibly coming to terms with the fact that his release would come much later than he would like. My hips and his cock moved in circles, like a dance...an increasingly pleasurable dance. My orgasm came very fast and very hard, and Derek groaned, begging me to let him cum. He was trembling with want so I let him slide his cock into my pussy. He felt so large and so good inside me, and when I gave him permission, he began to pound away like it was his salvation. His eyes rolled back into his head from the sensation coursing through his body.

"May I cum?" he asked, like a small child asking for sweets.

"Yes, my pet," I murmured. "In your hand."

No sooner had I murmured those words than he withdrew his cock and spilled his seed into his hand, trembling and calling out my fake name. He remained there on his knees between my legs, his chest heaving from his exertion and in relief.

****

Now, the office was another interesting place to look for a man that was into my kind of play. The only disadvantage was that I was stuck giving them my real name if they were colleagues. An advantage that countered that disadvantage was that the men I found were almost always clients. And that came in handy, seeing as I worked as a media consultant for an advertising agency.

All I usually had to do was sit in my office and allow the client to come to me. I would ask them about their personal life under the guise of it being business-related, while I assessed them from the outside; their demeanor, body language, dress style, and of course, their ring finger. If a ring was absent, I asked them questions that would reveal if they had a woman in their life. I always encouraged them to overshare. I mean, what better way to know them?

When I saw the lust in their eyes as they regarded me, I asked them straight up, "This is not business-related, but would you do me?"

The response I got was about eighty-five percent positive. Then I weeded them out with more questions. I rose from my chair and perched on the desk in front of them, slipping my foot from my shoes and placing it on their crotch, caressing them. Showing them what they would be missing out on if they refused.

"How well do you take orders?" I'd ask them. They were always eager to demonstrate right away, but of course, not all of them made the cut. Only a select few got invited to my love nest.

***

Sometimes I like to take the bus home. Not because I have any need to take it, but it made for an interesting hunt. And sometimes, I simply took the bus without any destination in mind. Like that one summer afternoon I met one of the men I stayed the longest with:

When I got on the bus, quite a number of eyes were on me. I was wearing a mustard yellow printed maxi dress with a dipped neckline. There was a good amount of skin on display. My eyes were hidden behind dark sunglasses for discreet scanning. I walked down the narrow bus aisle to the empty seat I spotted in the back. I avoided men with headphones on, and men that gave me overly lascivious looks—those usually came from older men and those that could never submit to a woman.

Not finding anyone interesting, I took my seat and brought out a book, pretending to read. In truth, I studied every new man that got on the bus. A quite attractive man came in through the front.

There were empty seats he could have taken, but he made a beeline for me, as though he knew me. He took a seat beside me, introduced himself and we got to talking. He got off the bus with my card.

He came over every week and at first, we had a lot of fun together; he loved being gagged and whipped. But as the weeks passed, he began to want me to be more than just his dominant mistress. He gave me gifts, which I rejected, because accepting them would mean more demands from him. I was in control here, and no one was going to take that from me. You see, needy men were the reason I didn't use my real home or my real name. My freedom to explore my desires without commitment was paramount.

***

Like most women, I get taken out on dates to nice restaurants, and on some evenings, I take myself out. On this evening, I donned on a sparkling emerald green dress with a deep V neckline.

I sat at a table, enjoying the atmosphere and a glass of wine. There were couples, friends, and work associates occupying most of the tables. Nothing out of the ordinary, but then something caught my eye.

I spotted a man sitting alone at a table for two, constantly checking his watch and throwing anxious glances at the entrance. He had the frustrated look of someone being kept on ice.

Like the hunter that I was, I walked over to his table and asked if the seat opposite him was taken. Unlike all the other men I'd met, this one was not surprised at my approach. He had a quiet look to him and his body was smaller than what I was used to, with a bone structure I could only describe as delicate. I instantly liked what I saw.

"So, what are you doing here all by yourself?" I asked, refilling his glass with more wine.

"I had a date. She stood me up." He shrugged, trying to hide his disappointment.

"First date?"

"Yes."

"Did you plan on fucking her tonight?" I asked, not minding my language.

"If she let me," he replied, a small smile playing across his face.

"Would you fuck me instead?"

He straightened at that. "How can I refuse a woman this beautiful?"

Now was the time to ask that final question that tipped them over the edge and into my world.

"Would you let me fuck you?"

He was quiet for a long moment, his face unreadable, but I could guess what he was thinking. He was weighing the cons and benefits of having a woman dominate him. They always did that when they went quiet in deliberation.

Finally, he said, "Do you want to get out of here now?"

I grabbed my purse without a word and made for the door. He followed me, guiding me to where he parked his car.

I made him stop at a street-side pastry shop for a cake.

Once inside the apartment I designated for my pleasures, I took control and asked him to strip down. His body was hairless and he was slim. He was perfect. I sent him to the bathroom for an enema and a shower, then pulled him into a room and began dressing him. Deep red lingerie, a little black dress to show off those smooth legs and a brown wig.

I kissed his lips before applying lipstick on them, then stepped back to assess him. He looked pretty. Bending him over, I caressed his smooth butt before parting his cheeks to insert a plug. I needed him loosened up. He moaned as the plug penetrated his ass.

"Oh, you like that, bitch?" I asked, gently tugging his ear with my teeth. He let out another moan. I put a leather collar around his neck and attached a leash to it. Leading him to the living room, I ordered him to serve me that cake then feed me. I watched as he carefully placed a slice on a plate before coming over, his legs wobbling on stilettos to sit next to me. He forked small portions into my mouth, and I occasionally let him have a bite.

The remaining icing on the plate looked like it could be useful. I asked him to scoop the icing with his tongue and spread it over my pussy and my breasts, then lick them clean. I could tell he enjoyed it because he moaned with me in unison. His swollen cock protruded from his dress.

By now, my pussy was ready for a good pounding, but not from his cock. I strapped a vibrating dildo onto him and raised one leg over his shoulder. He slid the dildo in and I clutched the back of the couch for support, moaning for him to go harder and faster. The vibrator touched my cervix repeatedly, causing my body to erupt in one very long, very intense, orgasm.

After catching my breath, I pulled him by his collar to the floor where I made him get down on all fours. Hiking his dress up to his waist and pushing his panties aside, I strapped on the dildo he'd just fucked me with and removed the plug from his ass, adding more lubricant and sliding the dildo in.

He pushed his ass back for me to sink deeper and he cried out when I began to thrust faster, spanking him with my hands as I did. I could tell this was a life he was familiar with and enjoyed very much. If he kept up, he may just become one of my favorites.

I paused so he could turn around and face me while lying on his back. He spread his legs wide and I settled between them, sliding my vibrating cock back into his slick asshole. His swollen dick called to me, huge and rigid, and covered with pulsing veins.

"Take your cock in your hand and stroke it for me," I commanded.

He did as I asked, his face the very image of ecstasy. His mouth was wide open as his hands moved up and down his penis in lightning-fast strokes. His body went rigid, and an almost animalistic groan emanated from deep in his chest. It was one of the most fascinating things, watching his cock explode and spill, the semen shooting out in powerful jets unto my body.

He was beautiful, and I was definitely keeping him.

Story 6 - Pattie's Quest

Pattie, a young pretty girl, had just moved to the suburbs with her mother. Her father, who worked with a security firm in the city, had gotten into a dangerous tussle with a terrifying criminal ring.

"I promise it will just be for a little while and we'll be together again," Pattie's Dad had said, as he prodded her into the waiting car, bidding her goodbye with a kiss on her forehead.

Upon her arrival, Pattie looked at the foliage and flower hedges that surrounded her new home. She felt caged in and spent most of her days in her room.

She remembered with longing her boyfriend in the city. All the stolen moments of pleasure in the attic. She closed her eyes for a moment and imagined him begging to lick her as she spanked his naked butt until it turned a deep red. She moaned softly with her hands down her pajama pants as she lay in her new bed.

Pattie's eyes flew open as she heard a rustle in the bushes nearby. An unbelievably tall young guy with long black hair held in a ponytail on his head smiled at her shyly from the window and quickly cast his eyes at his feet. Pattie's belly roiled in excitement. It was the same handsome boy she had seen in her gym class at school. Did he stalk her all the way here? She wondered.

"Hello," Pattie pursed her lips and moved closer to him after rushing down the stairs and yanking the front door open.

"Hi. I...uh. I'm just," he paused to find the words. "My soccer ball," he stammered pointing at the ball on her front lawn. He always went mute in the presence of beautiful girls. As far as Pattie knew, he liked pretty girls, but was too shy to make a move on them. It thrilled Pattie that he couldn't even look into her eyes as he spoke.

He would be such an obedient sub, she thought to herself.

Pattie walked towards the ball and picked it up. Instead of bouncing it towards him, she held it under her arm.

"I will give you your ball back if you agree to play a game with me," she demanded with a grin.

He raised his eyes to meet hers. "What game is that?"

"First rule, you don't talk unless I tell you to," Pattie ordered.

He nodded.

Pattie felt like a boss bitch ordering him around, her panties getting wetter in excitement.

"What's your name?" she asked.

"Andy." He shifted on one leg and looked over his shoulder briefly.

She used her index finger to instruct him to follow her into the barn behind the house.

The barn was filled with old tools and was a bit dusty, but Pattie didn't mind getting dirty. She blew the dust off the table and sat on it. With her eyes fixed on his, she then pulled her top off to reveal a black bra with her full and round tits pressing to burst out. Andy sucked in a gasp.

She chuckled. "You like what you see?"

Andy nodded eagerly and licked his lips.

"Unhook my bra," she commanded.

Andy moved fast and got the bra off. He grabbed her boobs like a baby hungry for milk. Pattie's face clouded in anger.

"Did I say you could touch me?" she hissed.

"I'm... I'm sorry," Andy stammered.

"You have been a bad boy and must be punished," Pattie's lips curled. She spotted a horsewhip in a corner and drew it out. Andy's eyes widened in confusion.

"Pull down your shorts. Now!"

Andy stared at Pattie for a split second but rushed to obey. Pattie caught a glimpse of his huge bulge before he turned his naked butt to her, bending over with his hands on the wall. She licked her lips in delight.

Pattie lashed the horsewhip on his butt three times, and three red welts showed on his skin. Andy only twitched a bit, but no sound escaped his lips.

"Good boy. *Now* you may suck on my nipples," she said, slowly approaching him and turning him around.

Andy closed his eyes and ran his tongue over her nipples, giving her gentle flicks before sucking on her round tit.

"Stop!" Pattie yelled. Immediately, Andy obeyed, and she smiled. He was indeed a fast learner. She guided his face to her other breast, and pulled his hand up to pinch her nipple. Pattie felt his big cock straining against her thigh.

"Remove your boxers and hold your dick in your hands," Pattie ordered.

When he pulled out his dick, it was longer and thicker than she'd anticipated. She instructed him to jerk himself off, and he paused for a second, before immediately doing as she said.

"Faster, faster, faster!" she ordered, her eyes fixed on his massive cock.

Andy fastened his tempo until the veins in his head bulged and his eyes were rolling back in his head.

"Stop!" she commanded, just before he was about to explode in cum.

She smiled as she watched his body tremble as he struggled to control himself. Pattie raised her miniskirt up and pulled her G-string past her hips down to her knees. She pulled herself up on the edge of the wooden table behind her.

"Now, come here. On all fours. Like a dog."

Andy giggled and got on his knees. He crawled until he was in front of Pattie. She positioned his head between her thighs, spreading her legs wide open for him to feast on her cunt.

"Now, eat my pussy like you would your favorite ice cream. While you're at it, make loud noises like a billy dog, got it?

"Woof, woof," Andy barked, already in dog character.

Andy licked her clit first and worked his tongue along her labia, slowly going faster as Pattie squirmed in pleasure. He parted her parted lips and cleaned off all her juices with his tongue. With one finger inside her wet cunt, his tongue flicked her clit like his life depended on it. Pattie threw her head back and her groans grew louder until she squirted all over Andy's face.

And then she heard her mom calling her from the house.

"My parents are home!" she whispered under her breath.

"Would you like to play this game with me again, Andy?"

"Yes, I would like to play with you every day," Andy gushed, thrilled.

They hurriedly got dressed. Pattie told Andy to wait in the barn until he heard a whistle from her signaling that the coast was clear for him to leave. He gave her a deep bow as she exited the barn.

***

Pattie and Andy were seated on the dining table, distracted by their art class project. But Pattie couldn't help but stare at Andy's long fingers. They were skillful at arts and crafts, and even better at pleasuring her body. Pattie's mom had been relieved to see her daughter make friends in their new neighborhood, as she had been verbal about being how upsetting it was to leave the city and her friends behind.

Pattie's mom came into the room with a tray of chocolate chip cookies. She smiled as she watched them busying themselves with their school work.

"Here are some cookies to chomp on after all that work. There's some apple juice in the fridge, too," Pattie's mom said, as she picked her car keys and walked to the door.

The moment they heard her mom's car pulling out of the yard, they both froze and exchanged glances.

"Remove your clothes!" Pattie ordered.

Andy stripped and waited.

Pattie got up and rummaged through the kitchen cabinets before she came back with a collar with a long leash. She secured it around Andy's neck and motioned for him to get on all fours before she guided him into her room. With a sinister grin looking down at him, she ordered him to lie on his back as she stood over him. Andy's eyes danced in excitement, his dick instantly going hard, begging for attention.

"Do you want me to fuck you?"

"Yes, please mistress. Fuck me hard and make me scream," Andy begged.

From the look in his eyes, Andy likely expected Pattie to jump on his dick and ride him. Instead, she moved to her dressing mirror and squeezed out some lube on her fingers. His eyes widened, confused.

Pattie then got on the floor behind him, where he stood on all fours. She spread out his ass cheeks until his tight hole was in clear view. Andy was already twitching to her touch. Slowly, she inserted her index finger into his hole. Andy gasped as she began to move her fingers in and out in a slow rhythm.

"Do you like that?" Pattie asked.

"It...it feels different," Andy stuttered.

Pattie gradually went faster and Andy moaned. Pausing for a moment, she slipped in a second finger and continued to finger-fuck his hole, and this time, much more vigorously. When she tried to stuff in a third finger, he let out a raspy moan in a mix of pleasure and pain. Using her other hand to stroke his balls, Andy moaned and muttering something unintelligible, likely asking for her permission to cum. But she wasn't about to grant that. Not yet.

His eyes were closed tightly. And just when he was about to cum, Pattie stopped.

Andy's eyes flew open, tears forming in the corners. "Please, don't stop, mistress. Please," he begged.

Pattie smiled. "Patience, little doggy."

She opened a drawer and brought out a lace garter, a feather whip and silver cuffs. Pattie had stolen the cuffs from her father's office, on one of the few days he allowed her to visit him at work. The feather whip, on the other hand, was a keepsake from her former boyfriend.

Andy's eyes showed terror and excitement simultaneously as he watched Pattie's movements.

She pulled him up from the floor and pushed him on the bed, cuffing each of his hands to the bed stand. Then, she took her time to undress as he watched her like a lappy dog waiting for a bone snack. Her nipples became dark and erect. She wore the garter and slipped into a pair of red stilettos that she pulled from under her bed. She climbed on the bed with the feather whip in hand.

Pattie lashed the feather whip on Andy's cock, and he winced sharply. He had never felt anything like that before. He wanted to cry and giggle at the same time. She whipped his dick in a fast frenzy, and when he was overwhelmed by the pain, she began to stroke his cock with the feathers. His dick became rock hard and he moaned.

"Please, mi-mistress. Fuck me hard," Andy begged.

Andy began to moan, as a trickle of tears flowed down his cheeks. He strained against the cuffs, yearning to be able to touch his dick, but he couldn't. He begged with eyes in full submission to Pattie.

Pattie squatted on her stilettos and sat on his dick. She rocked back and forth very fast and then slowed down her motions into a circular movement that set Andy crazy.

"Say my name," she screamed, as she went faster and faster.

"Mistress, mistress, mi-" Andy screamed with his eyes rolled back.

Just as he was about to cum, Pattie pulled his cock out of her and began to whip his dick with the feather whip. Andy was sweating hard, his face turning red as he screamed even louder. His cum exploded, splashing on the wall, and some on Pattie's thighs.

"Thank you, mistress," Andy said, breathless.

***

Pattie was disappointed with Andy.

She had seen him flirting with one of the cheerleaders in school. From the looks of it, it was actually the girl making the first approach but Pattie was still angry that he stayed there, enjoying the attention.

"I'm so sorry, mistress. She was all over me, and I tried to push her away," Andy pleaded.

"I didn't see you moving away from her. You just stood there staring at her boobs!" Pattie fired back.

Andy stared at his feet, his hands fidgeting.

"You have been a bad, bad doggy, and you will have to be punished!"

"I understand, mistress."

With that, Pattie dragged Andy into her room. She dug into her lingerie drawer and brought out pink lacy panties with a matching bra. Then, she moved to her shoe rack and pulled out black stilettos.

"Take off your clothes and put these on," she ordered monotonously.

Andy stared at the items in confusion. He put on the bra and hooked it with no troubles. The next hurdle for him was the stilettos, which were too small for his feet, but Pattie insisted he slipped into them halfway. Finally, Pattie shot him one long look, and put on some music.

"Now, dance for me, slut!" Pattie ordered.

Andy tried to twist his waist and wave his hands but his lack of balance on the heels sent him crashing to the floor.

"You clumsy whore! Get on your feet and dance!" Pattie commanded.

Slowly, Andy got up and balanced himself until he stopped wobbling, swaying to the music seductively. Pattie moved toward him and painted bright red lipstick on his lips, before dabbing some of it on his cheeks. He was gorgeous.

"Now get on your knees and suck my toes," Pattie spat. She settled into a chair and placed her feet on a stool. Andy carefully massaged each toe, and licked one after the other.

"Pull your dick out and whip it around like it's doing a dance."

Andy followed Pattie's instructions to the letter. As he whipped his dick around, it began to get hard. The veins stood out. Andy's eyes began to shut in pleasure.

"Don't you dare cum now!" Pattie warned.

Andy's eyes flew open and he quickly controlled himself.

"I will only cum when you give me permission."

Pattie ordered him to pull down the pink panties to his knees and bend over, his balls dangling between his legs. Pattie scanned over her room, looking for something that could serve as a makeshift dildo.

"Spread your legs wider," Pattie commanded.

Andy did as she said and waited. He was not allowed to look back at what she was doing. Finally, she saw just what she needed. Her purple, slim and well-rounded hair curler. She pressed out some lube onto the tip and walked eagerly to Andy, who still stayed obediently in position.

"Are you ready to be fucked until you scream for more?"

"Yes, mistress. Please take me, I'm all yours," Andy responded.

Pattie used the curler's end to tease around his asshole for a bit. He tried not to move, but he wriggled. She pushed it slowly inside his hole until it was almost halfway in.

"That's for being a naughty boy!"

"I'm sorry, mistress."

The sound of Andy's moans made Pattie dripping wet, but she wasn't going to let him touch her until he had served his full punishment. She slid the curler in and out, going faster and deeper. When Andy began to scream in pleasure, Pattie stuffed a dirty sock in his mouth.

"Thank you, mistress."

Pattie decided to stop just at that moment. She ordered him to sit down and watch her. She unzipped her dress and allowed it to fall at her feet. Andy looked on hopefully, his dick throbbing as he waited to be fucked hard.

But Pattie did exactly the opposite of his expectation. She sat and opened her legs wide and dipped a finger into her wet pussy. She lifted up her finger to his nose so he could smell her scent before she shoved it into his mouth to lick it off. He hungrily obeyed.

"Please, let me pleasure you, mistress," Andy begged.

"No, you have been naughty so you only get to watch," Pattie said, a wicked smile playing around her lips.

Andy groaned, as if in pain. Pattie slid another finger in her pussy and began to fuck herself vigorously, her eyes fixed on Andy's. She squeezed a nipple with her other hand and fingered herself even faster. Her juices began to drip and Andy licked his lips in anticipation. Pattie continued to touch herself until she reached an orgasm, and her body shook in ripples of pleasure. Andy's face crumpled up as if he was about to cry.

"I'm sorry, mistress. I'm so sorry," he pleaded.

"Shut up! Come here and clean this mess off my pussy."

Andy rushed to Pattie and she told him to lie on his back. She lowered herself onto his face and swiveled her hips. He slurped and licked her up loudly just like she loved it.

"Yeah, just like that! Good boy!" Pattie moaned.

Suddenly, the door flew open. Pattie's mom screamed in shock. "What the hell?"

Pattie rushed to her feet and covered herself up. Andy hid behind her, trembling.

"You vile creature! What are you doing to my daughter?" Pattie's mom yelled.

Pattie blocked her mom from reaching Andy as he stood with his hands covering his dick.

"Mom, he didn't do anything I didn't want. I made him do it," Pattie said.

Surprisingly, Pattie's mom stopped in her tracks. She stared at her daughter like she was just seeing her for the first time. "So, *you* are the one in control here?" she asked for confirmation.

"Yes, mom and you're embarrassing us. Please leave my room."

Andy couldn't believe his eyes as Pattie's mom turned to leave. She stopped at the door and said, "Pattie, we are going to have the mummy and daughter talk later, okay?"

Pattie nodded.

"Wow, your mom is a strange one. Mine would have burst a nerve if she'd walked in on us," Andy whispered, still in shock.

"Well, I guess she knows I won't stop and I'm not really a baby anymore. So, Andy would you like to continue from where we stopped?"

"Yes, mistress!" Andy crooned.

He knelt before Pattie and sucked her clit as if his life depended on it.

Story 7 - Online

I sighed as I stared at the crowd of faces in front of me.

My eyes were glued to my phone as I leaned back into my desk chair.

Swipe right, swipe right, swipe left.

I had just downloaded an online dating app at the suggestion of a good friend of mine at work. Having been single for the last couple of years, I was starting to wonder if I was ever going to find love - in person, or online.

It wasn't that I had a problem getting dates; I'd gone to a couple already this year. After all, I was a decently attractive guy. I was average in weight and build, a fair-sized dick and a steady job. Sure, I wasn't anyone's dream boy, but I wasn't all too shabby and I frequently got lucky – so to speak.

But the problem was never the kind of girls that I had dated. The problem was me.

I sighed again, my eyes drifting from the phone and landing on the computer screen in front of me.

In front of me were pictures of beautiful women – goddesses - dressed in latex and leather, standing tall and proud in their high-heeled boots.

I felt a stirring in my pants. *Damn, they're gorgeous!*

I wanted more than your typical vanilla relationship. I wanted more than the occasional fuck after a long day of work, before cuddling up in bed and redoing it every other night.

I wanted to feel the sting of a beautiful woman's big rubber dildo inside of me. I wanted to kneel at her feet, my cock hard and ready, worshiping every inch of her.

I craved the feeling of sharp nails digging into my skin as she would grab my hair and pull my face against her pussy.

I shuddered, the arousal spiking through me like a drug.

I thought about putting down my phone and giving up for the night. My body was thundering with arousal and there were many sites that I could visit. I could live out my fantasy, if only for a moment...

Ding!

A message on my phone dragged me away from my fantasy woman and back into the real-world of online dating.

I glanced at the app and clicked, skimming the message.

I smiled. Jessica. A beautiful girl with thick black hair and deep-set eyes. She had full red lips in her profile picture, and I couldn't help but admire her curves, the way her waist nipped in around her full hips.

I bit my lip, wondering what it would be like to bend over the bed and have her plow me from behind.

I shook away the intrusive thoughts, my dick twitching in my pants. Focusing instead on the conversation, we got to chatting.

Jessica was nice. She seemed sweet and funny, and we hit it off straight away. Our texts were mostly about the kinds of trivial things that people spend their days talking about. Favorite movies and work and whatnot.

Turns out, we had a lot in common. Plenty in common, actually.

I thought if we dated, it would be fun. It would be perfectly pleasant and sweet. Cuddling on the couch and brunching with our friends sounded like a good relationship in theory.

But I wouldn't be satisfied. And eventually, another relationship I get into right now would wither and die because I didn't have the courage to tell her what I really wanted.

I took in a deep breath.

I thought at least if I told her now, and she rejected me, it wouldn't be a drawn out and painful process.

My heart pounded in my chest.

I typed out the message slowly and carefully. I didn't want to come across as crass, but I wanted her to know where she stood with me right off the bat.

Jessica, you seem great. But before we do anything else, I wanted to be upfront with you. I'm not looking for a vanilla relationship. I'm looking for something more, for a mistress who isn't afraid to have her way with me, I paused to revise my text, then pushed send and held my breath.

For a few moments, I didn't get a reply.

Then she hit me.

Jessica: *WTF? What the hell is wrong with you? What kind of sicko creep would be into that twisted shit?* she wrote back.

I felt my heart sink into my stomach.

I made to type something, to apologize, only to see that Jessica had signed off the app. She clearly wasn't interested in talking to me anymore, not after what I had said.

I felt my stomach twist.

I had never had the courage to be open with a girl before, and my first attempt had been hit with flat-out rejection. I felt my arousal die in my pants and I flicked off my computer monitor and turned off my phone.

I needed a drink. And then I needed to go to bed.

Maybe the world of online dating wasn't all it was cracked up to be. Maybe it was no different from the conventional dating that I was used to. Disappointing and unfulfilling, no matter how fucking hot that girl was.

***

When I got home from work the next day, I was tired. My body was aching and I was exhausted from spending an entire day standing and rushing back and forth.

After a quick shower and a microwave dinner, I felt a little bit better. But my mind was still echoing that conversation I had last night, over and over. I couldn't get Jessica out of my mind.

"Never going to happen," I muttered to myself, making my way to my bed and throwing myself on it. I grabbed my phone after deciding that I was settling in for the night, and maybe watch some videos to amuse myself.

Ring, ring!

When my phone buzzed in my hand, I nearly dropped it in surprise.

I glanced at the number, but I didn't recognize it. For a moment, I hesitated.

Then I picked up.

"Hello?" I answered.

"Shh, don't speak," a sexy, sultry voice answered. There was a hard, firm edge to her voice that sent shivers down my spine.

I obeyed.

"You're going to listen to me, and you're going to do what I say. If you don't, I'll hang up right now," she said before pausing for a few moments, likely enjoying the sound of my heaving breaths. I couldn't believe what I was hearing, and I couldn't stop hyperventilating. "You're free to hang up whenever you choose, but if you do, I won't be in touch again."

I felt a shiver move through my body. I waited in bated breath.

Could it be? Was this what I had been waiting for?

"Speak only when I ask you a question. And you will address me as Mistress at all times. Do you understand?"

Oh god, yes.

"Yes, Mistress," I said, feeling the excitement pound through my body.

My body was humming with desire.

I reached over to my bedside drawer and pulled out my things. As she suggested, I kept a stash of toys and other things in my nightstand.

"I want you to grab your biggest toy. That buttplug that you use when you're feeling especially slutty," she said, her voice a low purr.

It was almost as if she was here in the room with me.

I grabbed the toy out of my nightstand drawer, feeling the girth and width of it. I shivered. It was heavy and weighty, and I couldn't remember the last time I had played with it.

"Got it?" she asked.

"Yes, M-mistress," I stammered, feeling the heat rise to my cheeks.

"Good boy," she said.

My cock twitched with lust.

"Now, I want you to get it nice and slick for me," she said. "I want you to lick it and suck it. Pretend it's my big, thick strap-on, and suck it really good for me."

She paused, and I could hear the wickedness in her voice. "Make sure you're on your knees."

I blushed, feeling the warmth of the blood rushing through my veins. I knelt to the ground, my knees hitting the carpet. My cock was hard as I lifted the big, black butt plug to my lips.

My cock was aching with need as I started sucking it, licking and flicking it with my tongue.

"Push it in deep." She purred and I did.

I gagged as I pushed it down my throat and started drooling. I closed my eyes, moaning as I sucked on it, imagining her beautiful face looking down at me, grabbing my hair as she thrust her plastic cock into my mouth and down my throat.

My hand moved to my dick instinctively. I wanted to cum so badly, and I hadn't even touched myself yet.

"You better not be touching yourself, you little slut," she said, a stern edge to her voice.

My eyes flew open, as though I thought I would see her in the room with me.

She was reading me so well. I felt a shiver run down my spine, reluctantly dropping my hand. I squeezed it into a fist, trying to ignore the need that was thundering through my body, the desire to grab myself and stroke hard.

I couldn't remember the last time I wanted to cum so badly.

"Is it good and wet, yet? Don't stop sucking until I say you can," she barked.

"Mhmm," I moaned around the gag, which was muffled as I continued to suck on the toy.

"Good boy. Alright. I want you on the floor, bent over on all fours. Take that toy and push it all the way down your ass."

Her voice was warm and soft, but the hard edge was hiding just beneath the velvety tones. I loved it. I didn't know who she was, but right now, I didn't care. It was like I had found my perfect domme – or rather, she had found her way to me, which made it even hotter.

"Yes, Mistress," I said quickly, scrambling to get on all fours beside the bed. My dick was throbbing as I bent over, lifting my ass into the air.

My breathing was quick. I was frantically panting like I'd just run a marathon. I could feel my heartbeats pounding in my chest, completely overwhelmed by my arousal.

"As you're pushing it in, I want you to play with yourself a little," she purred. "Stroke your cock, jerk off until you feel yourself teetering on the edge....and then I want you to stop." Her tone was sinister and sexy. I had no clue what she had waiting for me, but I knew for a fact it was going to torment me.

"When you're close to cumming, I want you to beg me," she commanded. "You don't get to cum until I say so. You ask for my permission," her voice hardened. "If you don't, you'll never hear from me again."

I shuddered. That would be the worst outcome. I wanted to hear her voice again and again. I wanted to serve her and be her personal slave. I couldn't afford disobey her, even though I knew it was just over the phone.

"I promise I'll ask first, Mistress," I said, breathless as I lifted the toy and pressed it gently against my entrance.

"Good boy," she purred, her voice softening. "Now be a good little slut and fuck yourself with that big cock."

I moaned as it started to slide down my ass. I was more relaxed than I'd expected to be, but my throbbing cock was probably distracting me from the burn. I trembled as I pushed it deeper and deeper inside me, the ache between my legs reaching a fever pitch.

I leaned forward so that my face was pressed against the carpet, my legs spread and my ass was in the air. I slid one hand between my thighs and started to stroke my cock. My hand had never felt so good. I imagined that it was her wrapping her fingers around my hard cock, playing with it and toying me, making me beg.

My whole body was vibrating with pleasure, and I was panting now, hard and fast.

The toy, slick with my spit, was sliding easily into my needy, wanting hole.

"Are you taking it really good for me?" she purred.

"Yes, Mistress," my voice shook, trembling over the last word.

My cheeks flushed with pleasure and I bucked my hips into my hand, thrusting my aching dick as I stroked it. I felt like I was about to explode.

I moaned loudly.

"You better not cum without my permission," she snapped.

"I won't, Mistress, I won't..." I moaned, trembling.

I could feel it building within me, the pleasure clouding my vision and leaving me breathless, trembling, and needy.

I had needed this for so long, a woman who knew what she wanted, who knew how to dominate me and leave me feeling wanton and needy, like the desperate little whore that I was.

"Oh god!" I gasped, my breathing shaky as the toy that slipped all the way in.

I was frantically stroking myself off, my cock hard and dripping pre-cum. I didn't know if I could hold on for much longer.

"Mistress, can I cum?" I gasped, the words leaving me in a rush.

Suddenly, I didn't give a damn that I was begging to a stranger, with a toy pushed in my ass and my cock in my hands. I just wanted to cum. I just needed to cum so badly.

"No," she said.

I could hear the smile in her voice, playing on her lips, "You haven't begged me enough."

"Please, Mistress," I moaned. "Please let me cum." I gasped, my head growing heavier.

"Not yet," she purred. I could tell she was enjoying this, and it just made my arousal all the stronger.

"If you want to cum, you're going to have to give me your address," she said.

For a second, I was confused. My lust-fueled mind was struggling to keep up. "What?" I asked.

"Your address," she insisted. "These games are fun on the phone, but I won't let you cum until I get to see you in person." There was a pause. "Or, you can walk away right now, and never hear from me again."

"No, no..." I gasped. I rattled off my address, the words leaving my lips before I had a chance to think about it.

"Good," she said. "Do you have self-bondage cuffs? Lockable ones?"

"Y-yes, Mistress," I sighed.

"Good. I'm going to hang up and you're going to unlock the front door. Then you're going to put on your collar, your blindfold and your cuffs," she said, calm and confident. "You're going to kneel in the entryway, and you are going to wait for me." She stopped for a second. "And leave the buttplug in."

Then she hung up, leaving me confused and desperate.

I wasn't thinking straight, but her orders echoed in my head. I grabbed everything that was needed, groaning at the buttplug filling me. Shortly after, I did as I was told, not even sure why I was trusting a stranger. I unlocked my door. I put on my collar and blindfold. I slid my hands into my cuffs and locked myself up, hands behind my back. Vulnerable. Helpless.

Although a little scared, I knelt at the front door with my legs spread. My cock was hard and erect, begging for release.

Right now, I knew I would do anything that she told me to do. Silence passed for what felt like an eternity. And then I heard it. The creek of my front door clicking open. The sound of heels on the floor and the sound of the door shutting behind me. My whole body was shaking.

I heard a soft release of breath.

"Such a good little slut, obeying his Mistress," her voice, smooth as silk, echoed throughout my home.

She was here with me, no longer just a voice on the phone. She was really here.

I heard her approach me even further.

"Looks like you didn't cum without permission," she purred. I heard the rustle of fabric as she shifted, her breath ghosting my face ever so slightly.

I didn't dare speak.

"Do you want to cum?" she whispered. I felt her breath in my ear, and I shivered, my cock twitching.

"Yes, Mistress." I moaned.

Her hand circle my dick, her grip gentle and firm. Her hands felt so soft, and I whimpered.

"Then fuck my hand. Work for it, whore," she said, her words harsh, but her voice soft.

I was shaking, the arousal so desperate that I couldn't see straight.

Unthinking, driven by lust, I obeyed. I thrust into her hand, moaning as I did. She felt so good. I bucked into her hand, moving my hips as I slid across the silky skin of her palm.

"Mistress.... Mistress, please..." I moaned, "Please, let me cum."

Right now, all I could think about was the need. All I could think about was the burning passion between my thighs. I needed this. I needed her.

My hands, bound behind my back, were useless to me. It was one thing to beg her when it was my own hand on my dick. But now, all she had to do was step away, and I would be left thrusting into the air, unable to find relief.

Now, my begging had a more urgent, desperate tone to it.

"Mistress, please," I whined, whimpering as I thrust. I knew I must look pathetic and desperate, humping her hand and begging, but I didn't care. I needed relief too badly to care.

"Please, please, Mistress. Please, let me cum!" I gasped.

I couldn't take it anymore. I was so close.

"Cum, my little slut," she permitted.

I obeyed, my body shaking with an earth-shattering orgasm. My legs were shaking, my body trembling as I came, the pleasure rushing through me in great big waves. For a moment, I couldn't do anything but pant and try to catch my breath.

Everything felt so good, so sweet, so electrifying as the pleasure raced through my body.

"Good boy," she said, and I could hear the smile in her voice. I longed to see her.

There was silence for a moment before she spoke.

"So, I was lying about... submissive men turning me off," she confessed.

She reached forward and gently pulled back the blindfold. I blinked, adjusting to the light.

Jessica was standing in front of me, a seductive smile on her face, wearing the most drop-dead gorgeous dress I had ever seen.

"I just needed to know that you could... really commit," she explained. "Turns out, you might just be the perfect slave for me."

She reached down and squeezed my cock, and I winced before a smile dawned on my face.

My dream woman was standing right before me.

Story8 - Natalia's Slave

The night I thought my, then, fiancée was going to leave me was the night our relationship completely transformed – the night I became Natalia's slave.

We'd met three years ago. Although it had never been said, I knew that I could fulfill her every need, except perhaps, any that were sexual. Beautiful as she was, she always wanted me to take control in bed, which was a role I could never fit. And of course, sporting a six-inch cock and finishing in fifteen minutes wasn't exactly impressive, especially not for a gorgeous woman like Natalia.

While I knew we were mutually happy with each other, I couldn't afford to lose her to someone who could pleasure her better. The offense would just add to the heartbreak.

But even though we have known each other for years, there was a lot that was left unsaid, and a lot that I hid from her lest she find me perverted. She had tits the size of cantaloupes and a round ass I could have for supper any day, but there was always something about her feet that instantly made my cock hard just thinking about them. Just a single glance at her slender painted toes and all sorts of flashing images of sucking on them would run before my eyes.

But I never dared bring it up. Not until that night.

She cooked us dinner after telling me that "we needed to talk." The words had struck me like a blow. This was it. She was going to leave me for some douchebag with a ten-inch that could dick her down for hours. As she set the table, her smile appeared forced and uneasy. She leaned over the dining table to light the three candles set in the antique tabletop chandelier, her braless tits bobbing with her every movement. I feigned a smile as we sat down and played with my food until she broke the silence.

"Michael," she began. "I don't know how to tell you this."

I knew it. She was leaving me. The hottest and most intelligent woman I've ever met was done with me.

"But you're kind of a lousy fuck," she continued casually with a perfunctory nod.

Wait. What?

"I know, I shouldn't have waited three years to tell you this, but you really are disappointing in bed."

"So, you're not leaving me?" I finally shook off my shock.

"What?" No!" she scoffed. "I love you, but we need to be," she paused to search for the right words. "Less vanilla."

There was a long silence.

"I mean, do you not have any fantasies?" her tone was suggestive, but was otherwise laced with a sense of authority that has always turned me on.

I impulsively glanced at her toes under the table. She wore black flip flops, which nicely contrasted the bright red nail polish on her toenails. My throat bulged as I swallowed hard, my gaze shifting back to her face.

"Michael?" she waked me from my daze.

I cleared my throat. "I don't know."

"Really?" she asked sarcastically. "So," she paused, glancing at her own feet. She kicked off a slipper and beckoned for me to follow her gaze. "There's *nothing* you've been wanting to do?"

This was the cue for me to finally come clean. "I worship your feet," I blurted out. The words came out more awkwardly than I initially planned.

She let out a soft chuckle, biting her bottom lip. "I know. It took you long enough to confess," she seductively chided, taking in a lungful of air. "So, show me," she beckoned softly, leaning back in her chair, her strawberry blonde waves covering one side of her face as her foot traveled up my shin.

She got up and slid the plates to the edge of the table, freeing up space to sit in front of me. Her tits bounced as she climbed up the table and eyed me down, her toes running along the inside of my thighs. As soon as her foot lightly pressed on the tip of my dick, I let out a deep exhale, my heart racing.

Natalia has always been a tease.

"May I?" I requested, my eyes fixed on her toes.

She nodded.

Gently, I grabbed her foot and motioned it to my mouth.

"Suck it," she commanded with her head held high, her expression emotionless.

At this point, I could no longer contain my arousal. I could feel a wet stain forming inside my sweatpants as she forced her toe inside my mouth and grinned and she watched me suck on it, momentarily stopping to give the rest of her toes a lick. I would stop every now and again to take a deep whiff of her divine scent, which made me all the more aroused.

"You're getting hard," she intoned, a soft chuckle edging her tone.

As her other foot caressed my cock over the thick fabric of my sweatpants, she leaned over to grab my neck, slowly pushing her foot all the way inside my mouth and against my throat. She pulled out her foot, and I gagged with a smile on my face. I was entranced.

I then followed her to the couch, where she ordered me to strip off, and I obeyed. She grimaced upon seeing my hard cock and fell back between the cushions of the couch comfortably. Slowly, she spread her legs, revealing her fat clit and flushed red cunt, which was dripping wet.

This was the start of a new chapter in our relationship – one that completely turned my sex life around.

* * *

What Natalia and I would have previously regarded foreplay now constituted our entire sex life. And neither of us had ever been happier.

While we rarely ever had intercourse, I spent most of my time with her worshipping her feet and eating her out. She wouldn't always allow me to come, but that made it sexier. Sometimes, she would fondle my dick with her feet and slowly jerk me off, but she would stop before I could finish and would instead make me tongue fuck her wet pussy with a throbbing dick.

But sadly, the daily oral session had to come to an end after I pinched a nerve in my neck at work. We both tried to find me comfortable position that didn't strain my neck, but I had to follow my doctor's orders, and I could thus barely move it left or right. I could only lie down on my back.

But knowing Natalia, she wasn't going to give up. Not after she'd made me into her little plaything.

We were getting ready for bed, Natalia reading a book beside me, while I was lying on my back. I heard her book slam shut before she tossed it over the bedside table. She slid down into the covers and turned to me.

"I'm glad treatment has been working out for you," she said softly, running a finger down my arm.

"I wish I could eat you out like old times," I confessed with a side smile.

"I mean," she said. "You still could."

"My neck," I reminded her.

"Don't move," she instructed.

Natalia sat up and climbed on top of me, grinding her pussy against my cock with her hands wrapped around the metal headboard bars. I let out a moan, unsure how this was going to end, but enjoying it nonetheless. She stiffened her grip on the headboard bars and pulled herself closer to my face until she mounted on it, sliding up and down to cover my skin in her juices. I could feel my cock throbbing as she finally settled atop my lips, spreading her labia with her fingers as her long hair tickled my chest every now and again with her movements.

"I love the way your face feels on my clit," she chuckled softly, then moaned as I began licking her clit.

She momentarily got up and spun around, leaning down ever-so-slightly before spreading her ass cheeks and continuing to glide up and down. "Lick my ass clean," she instructed.

I noticed that with time, her language and positions became far more dominant than when I'd first met her. She used to have a rather somber demeanor whenever we fucked, no matter how hard I tried to impress her, as if there was something missing. The entire time we dated, I'd become insecure, falsely thinking that she needed *me* to be more dominant and controlling.

Fortunately, I was mistaken.

With Natalia seated on my face, only briefly getting up to allow me to breathe, I knew *this* was the missing puzzle piece. She had always been a mistress at heart, and I was finally made into her little foot-boy slave. If she was seated on my face, mine was buried between her toes.

And with time, she began to make me beg for them.

* * *

On our anniversary, Natalia demanded that I take her to *The Hamlet* – the restaurant where we had our first date in our favorite booth by the window. The moment we walked in, I parted my lips to ask for our usual booth, but Natalia rushed to ask for a regular two-person table. I was confused by the gesture, but I didn't give it much thought. Granted, I was a little annoyed by how small the round table was until Natalia crossed her legs under the table and grinned at me.

Then I knew exactly what she had planned.

She shot me that devilish grin that I'd grown to admire, immediately putting me in slave mode. With her eyes fixed on me and her leg bouncing, she pushed her napkin off the table, the corners of her lips rising in a more seductive smile.

"Oops," she said, moving her foot in circles.

I returned the smile, bracing myself for a long session, for the first time, in public.

"Michael," she called out. "Why don't you be a dear fetch that for me?" Her voice was deep and sexy.

As soon as I pushed my chair back and leaned under the table, she let her heel drop, continuing to wiggle her toes to tease me. I kept thinking about how many people were probably looking our way right now, but I would quickly shake off the thought and take another whiff of her hypnotizing scent.

I froze. It felt as though there was no one else in the world but me and Natalia, with her feet sliding up and down my face, her toes stopping my lips from forcing them open. I could feel myself getting hard as Natalia looked down at me from above, grinning and biting her bottom lip.

"Will you be a dear and put my shoe back on?" she demanded, beckoning for me to get back down.

I obeyed, and soon as I sat back in my chair with my cock hard as a rock, the waitress put my plate in front of me, shooting my fiancée an approving smile. It looked like people other than Natalia had enjoyed the show that we put on display. Blood was still rushing through my veins, and I was still in a trance. I had no appetite for my meal, and only for Natalia, who motioned for the waitress to have my meal put in a doggy bag. The waitress shook her head with a wide smile on her face and nodded.

I'd thought that the teasing stopped there, but boy was I mistaken! She tossed me her keys and asked me to drive, instructing me to keep my eyes on the road no matter what happened. As I drove west on RT. 64 out of Carol Stream, I could see Natalia lifting her red dress and fondling her clit, letting out the sexiest deep moans I'd ever heard come out of a woman.

Difficult as it was, I followed her instructions and kept my eyes on the road, my throat bulging as I gulped. She let out that sexy laugh of hers and turned in her seat, her back reclining against the car door. She then proceeded to kick her shoes off, placing one leg behind my nape to secure my neck, and while her right foot made a beeline for my mouth. I could hear her the wet smacking noises of her finger sliding in and out of her wet pussy as she slid her foot back and forth, and made sure I nibble on each one of her toes before shoving her entire foot in my mouth.

To my left, a senior couple drove past us, and I could feel them gawking at us disapprovingly, making this all the sexier.

"You didn't eat much at the restaurant," Natalia noted, shoving her big toe inside my mouth as I sucked on it. "Are you hungry for anything in particular?" she paused to grin. "Something I can serve you when we get home?"

"I can't wait to go home and eat your pussy," I exclaimed.

She pulled her foot away and smacked me with it on the head. "What did we say?"

I cleared my throat. "May I please eat your pussy when we get home?"

"When we get home *what?*" she reminded me, her voice sending ripples down my naval and my cock hardening.

"Mistress."

She pulled her legs to herself as we pulled to the curb. "I'll think about it."

As soon as we stepped over the threshold of my house, and I kicked the door shut behind me, she grabbed my hand and led me to the living room sofa. "Lie down," she instructed, gesturing to the three-seater couch. I obeyed with a smile on my face, already anticipating what was about to happen. She kicked her shoes off with her eyes affixed on me, planting one bare foot on my crotch, and the other on my face.

I gasped, feeling my cock get hard again with her toes pressing against the rim, then sliding back and forth to lightly jerk me off. She shoved her toes in my mouth when I least expected, and I gagged a little as she pulled it out.

"Suck them," she ordered, wiping her foot all over my face and watching me try to catch them. She chuckled.

"Do you like my toes in your mouth?"

"Yes, mistress," I answered with a smile on my face.

"Is there anything else you'd rather have in your mouth?" she teased.

I nodded.

"Very well."

Gracefully, she climbed atop of me and let out a little sexy moan as she did. Her ass was on my chest when she unbuckled my belt and pulled my pants down, my cock immediately springing up. She smiled and slid backward, lifting herself to her knees on either side of my head. She was squatting on top of me with her long hair tickling my chest.

"Do you like what you see?" she moaned.

I swallowed hard and then nodded.

She wrapped her fingers around my neck. "What did we agree on?" she reminded me.

"Will you please sit on my face mistress?"

She lifted her head up, as though thinking about it, and she bit her bottom lip.

"Please, mistress. May I taste your juices?"

The corner of her mouth lifted in a side grin before she sat down on my face and began grinding. My nose was planted between her lips, and I couldn't breathe, but with Natalia sat on my face, I couldn't care less about oxygen when her pussy juices were dripping along my cheek. She grinded, twisted and turned, her moans like a sweet tune.

She rocked back and forth faster and faster as she grinded harder with her hand pulling her hood back, and her clit sliding side to side against the flick of my tongue until she squirmed and let out a long and loud groan, her sweet juices covering my face entirely. I'd always loved it when she came all over my face.

"I think my pussy's had enough attention," she announced, whipping her hair back. "I think my ass is getting jealous."

She placed her phone on my chest and backed her ass up until she landed on my face. With both of her hands, she spread her cheeks, and made me search her asshole with my tongue.

"That's it," she whimpered. "That's the spot. Lap it lightly."

I circled my tongue around her hole, memorizing the wrinkles and folds perfectly with a smile on my face. Once she was satisfied with the strokes of my tongue, she grabbed her phone from my chest and dialed a number. The phone rang a couple of times before a woman picked up.

"Hey, Chloe," Natalia said. "You still crying over that douchebag?"

I tried to pay little attention to the conversation she was having with her friend from cosmetology school, and instead focused on tracing her asshole with the tip of my tongue, lightly pushing just the tip of it inside her hole and quickly pulling it out. I was getting aroused and a little impatient, and I began to tongue fuck her little by little. Slowly, I pushed my tongue all the way inside her hole, and took a lungful of her scent. Natalia paused mid conversation and looked over at me.

"Did I give you permission to tongue fuck me?" she said with her eyes wide open. "Keep lapping. I'm not ready to be ass fucked yet."

I nodded and obeyed before she went back to the conversation she was having with her friend, casually and calmly.

By now, her friend had heard what she said and wanted to know what was going on, and without hesitating for a second, she told her exactly what we were doing – that she had been sitting comfortably on my face, and was about to further my training as her oral sex slave by teaching me how to perfectly worship her asshole!

Pulling away briefly from my face, she put the phone down next to my head and told me that her friend wanted to ask me a few questions, and I better tell her the truth or else.

"Yes, I understand," I said. "Hello?" I said to her friend.

"Is this true what Natalia just told me?" she laughed. "That she is training you to become an oral sex slave for her to use whenever she wants," she paused. "And that you are about to put your tongue inside her dirty asshole? Boy...you are one sick puppy! Why are you agreeing to do this?" she asked.

"Because, I love her and want to please her."

"I see. Well, let me talk to Natalia," she exclaimed.

"Okay my little ass-licker, here's what I want you to do," Natalia said. I want you to open your mouth nice and wide so that I can settle my pretty pink rosebud into your mouth. And when I am fully seated, and your lips are sealed around my asshole, I want you to start by softly licking, lapping and sucking away at my asshole. I want you to make love to my asshole with your mouth and tongue, got it?!"

"Yes, I understand."

I opened my mouth as her butt descended and settled onto my face once more, her asshole now imbedded deep into my mouth, and I began to do as I was told. Meanwhile, they resumed with their conversation.

"See? I told you I wasn't lying," Natalia said with amusement lacing her tone. "And yes, by the time I am through training him, he is going to be the best sex toy any girl has ever had!" She let out a chuckle "In fact," she continued, "If you'd be interested, why don't you come over sometime, and I'll show you exactly how pussy whipped he really is. Yes, I'm telling you...Michael is that good! He was born to lick and suck! So, why shouldn't I help him achieve his true destiny? Although, he sucks at fucking, with his tiny dick and all, he more than makes up for that with his talented mouth, and believe me, you can feel his passion with every stroke of his magic tongue," she paused to shoot me a glance.

"Oh, and he also has a foot fetish and loves to lick and suck on women's feet and toes, too! Yes! That's what gave me the idea to train him to be my complete oral slave...and my sex life has never been better! I can have as many orgasms as I want."

There was a pause.

"Yeah, I don't know...it's like he's addicted to licking pussy, and soon, I'll have him addicted to eating assholes, too! So, what do you say? Would you like to come over and watch me use him? Or better yet, why don't you join in and have a go on him yourself?" There was another long pause.

"Sure, I don't mind! In fact, it would turn me on to watch you using his face as he works his magic! So, what do you say? You would? Great! Did you hear that, ass-wipe? Soon you're going to have double the pussies and assholes to pleasure. Aren't you excited? This is going to be fun! Oh my gosh...I just farted on his tongue!" She chuckled hard, her voice echoing throughout the room. "I'm sorry dear, it was an accident," she stopped to continue laughing.

"Wow, he's acting like it didn't even happen! What? You want me to do it to him again...on purpose? Well, I don't know...I don't feel the need to. But, if I do feel one coming on, I'll be sure to let it fly!" Both she and her friend laughed in unison. "And judging from his reaction to the first one, I don't think he'll mind."

She wasn't wrong.

After she hung up the phone, she started to apologize again for farting, saying it truly was an accident. I assured her that things like that can and do happen from time to time, and that while it's humiliating and not very pleasant to experience on my end, I told her that I loved her no matter what.

Besides, I equated myself to being no different than any of the sex toys she had.

Soon, we went back to the main focal point of my training...her anus.

For about the next hour or so, I was to try and coax her flower to open up, to let my tongue enter that most sacred space. Then, once inside, she would clamp down on my tongue for a period of time, thus trapping me in place for a few seconds before releasing me. This was repeated for quite some time until her ring started to relax and stay open on its own. Now, it was time to insert my tongue as deep as I could get it, and to massage the inner walls of her rectum again and consequently, this aided in her releasing more gas, which I consumed.

Some were worse than others, but I endured it all.

I was then instructed to fuck her hole with my tongue and to try and get it deeper each time, which seemed like an impossible task and very painful indeed. On occasion, she would grip my tongue again and hold it inside her where she instructed me to wiggle my it around as best I could to add to her pleasure. And judging by the sounds emanating from her mouth and the slow humping of my face, I knew I was doing a pretty good job. And at one point, she would tighten up on my tongue that was buried inside her and go still and shudder, which I came to find out was her experiencing an anal orgasm.

By the time this session ended, she got off me and had me go brush my teeth and gargle with mouthwash, so that she could finish off the evening enjoying some much needed orgasms. I returned and assumed my position on the bed and noticed she had laid down some plastic sheeting and some towels upon which to lay my head.

As I got in position, she informed me that she had to pee, and since I did such a good job of consuming her gas, I shouldn't have much problem in drinking her golden nectar. With that, she lowered herself onto my face and told me to create a seal, this time around her pussy, which I did. At first it came out as a trickle, which was fairly easy to swallow. After that, it came out with more force, but she would pause once my mouth was full, where she commanded me to swallow. After a minute or two she was finished and instructed me to proceed sucking out the remaining drops, and to get to work in making her cum the first of many that night. At this point, I didn't know who was enjoying this more, her or me?

Every time she erupted in my mouth, I was lost in the thick, creamy goodness that was filling my mouth and flowing down my throat. I sucked, licked and gulped for all I was worth, trying to consume every single drop of her precious gifts. I could almost feel my body become weightless and one with her pussy, which owned me completely. Before she dismounted her seat for the night, she again, gifted me with a small drink of her golden nectar. After imbibing once again, I gently used my tongue to clean up any remnants of her gifts and softly kissed her pussy, signaling an end to the most exciting sexual experience of my life!

Story 9 - Justin's Humiliation

Justin had always liked to refer to himself as a closeted submissive.

He'd been tied up and spanked. Chained to the wall and had his balls slapped and wrung between a mistress's fingers. But all in his head.

He always fancied himself a good-looking man, but he wasn't exactly dominant in the bedroom. Although a handsome twenty-seven year old, he'd never had a partner for more than a couple of months. He was compassionate and kind, but perhaps too much so. All the women he'd randomly met over dating apps sought a dominant man in the bedroom, and he did as they pleased, but it was never fulfilling.

In fact, it was just the opposite of what he'd always craved: femdom humiliation.

Over the years, he'd gone through phases of porn and camgirl addictions, and although he was pretty much over them now, it wasn't because he put an end to it himself. On the contrary, they just weren't enough to satiate his deepest, darkest desires. He loved all women of all kinds of body types. His dream woman never had a specific appearance, but he always pictured her clad in latex with a paddle in hand.

How he'd wished for a woman to paddle his ass until it ached too badly for him to sleep on his back. His fantasies, to his best friend Kyle, were 'fucked up,' as he always put it. And eccentric as they may be, he promised him to find him his perfect woman for his birthday - or two.

Little did Justin know, his friend hadn't intended to hook him up with a friend of a friend. He was, instead, going to land him the highest-rated sex workers. Granted, Justin lived in Nevada, where brothels were always an option, but he never thought about paying for a woman to dominate him beyond the confines of a computer screen.

He lay in bed with his rubric cube, frantically turning one row after the other, with his eyes fixed on the ceiling. He ran his fingers through his blonde hair and let out a long sigh. Turning his head, he glanced at his phone on the bedside table, and hesitantly reached out.

Let me know if you wanna do this, Kyle's text read.

Justin clenched his jaw, pressed his eyes shut, then finally mustered the courage to type.

I've been thinking about this a lot. I'm not sure, he wrote.

Dude, you in or not? Celeste and Jasmine are waiting for a response. The discounted offer isn't gonna be on the table forever, his friend replied.

Are those even their real names? Justin's text read.

Does it matter?

No, let's do this.

* * *

Beads of sweat formed on Justin's forehead as he awaited the two women on his sofa. He kept shifting in his seat with his eyes on the ticking clock, already picturing what the women would look like. He licked his lips in anticipation and fell back in his seat. Before he could rest his head on the back of the sofa, the doorbell chimed..

He rushed to answer, the door squeaking on its hinges as he opened the door.

"You Justin?" one of the two women asked, vigorously chewing on her gum.

Both of them were clad in long black coats. One woman, whom he assumed was Jasmine, was taller than him, likely because she was wearing platform boots that may have been six inches. Her skin was dark and shimmery, her cheekbones accentuated by the porch lighting, and her voluminous afro was long enough to gracefully touch her shoulders. The other woman was shorter with a slight tan, her hair a dark shade of red. They both wore fishnet stockings and backpacks over their coats.

"Y-yes. That's me. Come on in," he invited them in with a wave of the hand.

As soon as he turned around to quietly press the door shut, he felt his body slam into the wooden door and he let out a shriek. Jasmine's hot breath beat down on his nape.

"Are you ready, you dirty fucking slut?" she whispered in his ear, her arms snaking around his hips and unbuckling his belt.

Boy, they sure as hell don't waste time, he thought to himself.

"Yes, mistress," he said submissively.

"Did I say you can call me mistress?" she hissed before landing a hard slap atop his jeans.

He jerked in place; the blow was far harsher than he'd anticipated.

"No," he answered before being turned around with force.

Celeste pulled his pants down and got on her knees.

"Take his boxers off, too," Celeste commanded her, and she acquiesced.

They both slid down the backpacks off their arms and let them fall to the floor.

Celeste was already fondling Justin's balls, albeit a little too harshly. Just as he liked it.

"Big ass balls on this one," she chuckled. "I didn't think he would be *that* pretty." She took a deep whiff of his already-erect dick. "Mmm," she moaned. "Let's see how you hold up.

As Celeste stripped off Justin from the rest of his clothes, Jasmine took off her coat and dropped it. Celeste followed as his back was still against the door. They were both clad in latex dresses, with their massive tits spilling out from the tight black bodice, bouncing with every move they made.

"Where do you want to start with him?" Celeste asked with a sinister grin, tilting her head ever-so-slightly. "Look at him," she scoffed. "He looks pathetic."

Jasmine searched the room left and right until her eyes landed on the dining table. She grinned and walked toward Justin, turned him around and grabbed him by his hair. His green eyes widened as he was shoved on the table and ordered to bend over.

"I love the way his balls look in that position," Celeste commented, joining Jasmine.

"I'd love to see the way they look after we're finished with him," Jasmine chuckled.

Justin's cheek was pressed on the table, and he could only hear their heels clanking on the wooden floor. One of them made her way to their bags and rummaged through them before pulling something out. As she slowly approached him, Justin twitched in anticipation.

From the way Celeste swayed the object, he could tell it was a massive whip. A small smile dawned on his face; his ass was ready for punishment.

"Spread your legs," Jasmine commanded.

Justin obeyed in a split second, moving slightly downward to free his hard cock, which was now erect under the table. He squeezed his eyes shut, awaiting the first blow. And just before he knew it, the whip strands landed on his balls, and he let out a surprised groan.

Both women let out chuckles. "Didn't think we'd go straight for the balls, did you?" Jasmine asked.

"No, mistress."

Fuck. She already told me not to call her that.

He heard her angry steps moving toward him before she grabbed him by the hair and pulled his head up, leaning down to his eye level and spitting on his face. "What did I fucking say about calling me mistress?"

"I'm sorry," he said.

"It's goddess," she corrected. She then gestured to her friend. "*She's* your mistress."

"That's right," Celeste echoed. "Now get back in position."

The blows were excruciating at first, but he soon adapted to the sweet pain and craved more of it as his cock throbbed in anticipation. He could feel his dick leaking, and he swallowed after every smack – counting every one of them.

"Twenty-five," he groaned, counting the last one.

"Not bad," Celeste praised. "Do you think he's ready for the next stage?" she asked her friend, sarcasm lacing her tone.

"Oh, you're bad," Jasmine said. "I like that."

From the sound of it, Justin could tell the women were kissing. He gulped, raised his head, and turned around to feast his eyes. But before he could, his eyes locked with Jasmine's furious glare.

"Did I say you could fucking move, slut?" she chided, the corners of her lips rising in a sinister grin. "Turn around!"

He obeyed and clenched his jaw as Celeste rummaged for another tool. This one was definitely made of metal. Jasmine, on the other hand, appeared to fetch her own toy. He was certainly in for the kind of humiliation he only saw in porn.

Justin recognized Celeste from the sound of her stilettos approaching him. She got on her knees and fondled his balls. He sucked a breath through his teeth in pain as she touched his sore testicles, a jab of pain coursing through his veins.

"Awh, does it hurt too badly?" Celeste snickered. "But we're just getting started with you."

Pain throbbed in his balls as Celeste coated them in lube before slowly forcing a steel ring around his swallowed testicles. He heaved a long and sharp sigh until the ring was secured at the base, making his member throb in pain. A moan escaped his lips as Jasmine continued to whip his ass, his body twitching and jerking with every blow.

"What do you say?" Jasmine called out, her whip landing on his ass once more, which was growing warmer and more sensitive to the touch with each lashing.

"Thank you, mistress," he said.

"Mistress?" Jasmine exclaimed furiously.

"Goddess!" he yelped.

The next blow was much harsher than the last, his hands quickly moving to his ass as a knee-jerk reaction.

"Move your hands!" Jasmine commanded. "Don't make me bust your balls again," she warned.

He slowly moved his hands, but not quick enough for the whip to land on his ass as well as his fingers. He let out a yelp and arched his back, overwhelmed with pain and pleasure. His cock was rock hard, and he felt it dripping precum. In a way, he was a little frustrated that he couldn't see the women, but the mystery made it all the more mysterious.

"Look what I found," Celeste announced. Justin had learned by now that looking back at them without their permission only granted him harsher punishments, and while he always looked forward to what they'd prepared next, he knew that his humiliation was only getting started.

Celeste walked toward him, landing her hand on the small of his back in a comforting gesture. Her hand slid downward, massaging his warm ass cheek, which was likely redder than their shade of lipstick by now. He twitched to her touch, then relaxed, her soft caresses soothing as well as arousing. She then lightly squeezed one cheek and gave it a pat.

"Good sub," she whispered under her breath.

His eyes widened upon hearing the bubbling noise of the lube tube being squeezed, his body jerking to the cold liquid upon landing on the small of his back. With a fingertip, Celeste massaged the lube along his ass, circling his hole and teasing it. He felt another hand on his balls, massaging it in circular motions, while still swollen inside the ring. He let out a long moan, which grew louder when Celeste finally pushed her finger all the way inside his asshole.

His mouth was agape, his body completely overwhelmed. While Jasmine stroked his hard cock and softly massaged his balls, Celeste was fingering his tight asshole, momentarily leaving her finger inside for a moment and massaging his prostrate in a slow and circular motion, before pulling it out half-way and repeating.

His cock was throbbing in Jasmine's hand. Leaning over to his eye-level, Celeste grabbed his face, with now two fingers inside his ass, and sucked a kiss out of his lips. She was a tease, biting his bottom lip and nibbling on it for a second before pulling away to watch the look on his face.

Justin felt himself getting closer to climaxing; he arched his back and began moaning louder.

"Not so fast!" Jasmine said, immediately letting go of his cock and balls, Celeste pulling away as well. "Don't you dare cum without my permission," she warned.

Celeste's finger began massaging his asshole again, but this time, she pulled away for a moment, because the chill of a metal butt plug made him twitch to the touch. She slowly eased it inside, and Justin moaned intermittently until it was completely secure inside his ass. He let out one long moan, then shrieked when the whip fell on his cheeks again. Each lashing would land on the plug, making him groan in pain before moaning in pleasure.

After he counted down ten lashings, the plug oozed out of his ass and made a clang as it fell to the wooden floor.

"I'm sorry," he moaned.

"Sorry, what?" Celeste prompted the right answer out of him.

"Sorry, mistress," he yelped.

"That's right," she said. "But do you know what that means?"

He shook his head.

Jasmine let out a chuckle. "It means, we'll have to try out something else. Something," she paused in suspense, "that you wouldn't be able to push out that easily."

Something much heavier was taken out of the bag.

"Help me put it on," Jasmine muttered, although loud enough for Justin to hear her.

And that's when he knew what was coming. Sweat dripped from his forehead and onto the table as the suspense tore at him. Was it really taking her that long to put it on, or were they torturing him with their silence?

And at last, he heard her walk toward him, yanking his hands from his sides and securing them to his back. With the tip of the strap-on, she circled it around his hole, teasing it every now and again, and chuckling every time he gasped.

"You're such a good little whore, aren't you?" she soothingly praised. "Not so much of a brat. My favorite kind."

Celeste rounded the table and stood where she could lock her eyes with him. She had stripped off her clothes, wearing nothing but her stockings. Her breasts were large and perky, and her nipples a little oversized, just the way he liked them. He could see that she was quite wet, and he couldn't help himself but grin.

But before the corners of his mouth could lift, he whimpered as he arched his back, Jasmine's plastic cock penetrating him all the way in. She thrusted in and out of him vigorously and swiftly, and he couldn't contain his screams.

"This will shut him up," Celeste said, rushing to climb the table. She sat on her knees, lifting his head by the hair and forcing his face to her wet pussy. She grinded and turned, softly moaning as he licked her clit in gentle flicks.

Jasmine pulled on his arms behind his back, which he arched, pushing his ass up in rhythm with her thrusts. He could feel tears forming in his eyes, his face completely covered in Celeste's cum. It was nothing like he had ever felt before. Many times he had been inside a woman, but he'd never had a woman fuck him in the ass before Jasmine did.

She pulled away and Celeste followed. They both exchanged glances and nodded. They were certainly up to something sinister, and Justin wondered what they could possibly have prepared next. His ass cheeks were red and sore, and his asshole was wide and ready for the taking. His chest heaved, rising swiftly up and down as he tried to catch his breath.

Jasmine stood between his legs on one side, while Celeste had her legs open above his face on the other, her knees on either side of his head. She lowered herself slowly, securing herself on his face with her lips spread open with her fingers. She gyrated her hips, grinding her clit on his lips before she slid forward.

"Fuck me with your tongue, you fucking slut," she commanded.

As Justin's tongue flicked Celeste's clit before gliding down to her cunt and penetrating her, Jasmine began sucking him off, using a little bit of teeth every now and again to watch him squirm. She flicked her tongue at the ridge, chuckling proudly when he twitched to the motion. She then slowly eased his member through her plump lips, and slowly shoved it down her throat, gagging and spitting on it every time she pulled away. Her other hand fondled his swollen red balls, which must have been hot to the touch. She gently pulled down the ring, and he let out a groan that was muffled between Celeste's wet pussy lips.

She slid the ring out completely and let it drop to the floor, and the relief he felt was nothing like he had ever experienced. He was close to climaxing, while Celeste, whose whimpers were growing into loud moans, seemed to also be close to orgasm.

She suddenly lifted herself up, and what followed was a stream of her juices squirting all over his face. Celeste then slapped him twice, then climbed down the table and pulled his head up through his hair, depriving him of the view of Jasmine sucking him off.

He was *so* close, his whole body shaking in anticipation.

"Goddess," he yelped, still twitching. "May I please cum, mistress?"

While he was seconds away from climaxing, Jasmine grinned after pulling his dick out of her mouth. He turned to his side and squirmed, shook, and twitched like a dying worm, realizing that orgasm deprivation had been part of his humiliation all along.

He was strangely aroused as well as frustrated, his dick seemingly leaking all the liquid there was left, but his cock was still throbbing.

Justin struggled to get up.

"Don't worry about it," Jasmine said, strangely out of character, as she began undoing her strap on. "It's already paid for."

Soon after, the two women collected their belongings and left without even looking him in the eye or saying goodbye. He sat up on the table with his eyes widened and his hands on his cock, a grimace dawning on his face.

His phone buzzed.

Happy birthday, Kyle's text read.